PIECES OF DREAMS

Maxine and Taylor found a great spot, dead center, with a perfect view of the concert stage.

Just as they began to eat their picnic dinner, the MC came on stage and the show began. For the next two hours, Taylor allowed himself to fall under Maxine's spell: her soft laughter, the alluring scent of her, the sparkle in her eyes, her witty observations about the people around them. And it wasn't that she was trying to win him over. Everything about her seemed natural, real.

About halfway through, Taylor had settled himself against a tree and eased Maxine against him, her back pressed against his chest. At first he felt her reluctance from the tightness of her body, the way she held herself ever so slightly away from him. But slowly Taylor felt her relax and let go, until resting against him seemed like the most natural thing in the world. Taylor pressed his chin against the top of her head and closed his eyes a minute, swaying just a little to the music.

Yeah, this is nice, he thought.

Other Arabesque Titles by Donna Hill

TEMPTATION
SCANDALOUS
DECEPTION
INTIMATE BETRAYAL
A PRIVATE AFFAIR
CHARADE
CHANCES ARE
MASQUERADE (Love Letters)
'ROUND MIDNIGHT (Winter Nights)
THE CHOICE (Spirit of the Season)

PIECES OF DREAMS

DONNA HILL

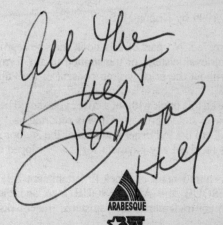

ARABESQUE
BET BOOKS

BET Publications, LLC
www.msbet.com
www.arabesquebooks.com

ARABESQUE BOOKS are published by

BET Publications, LLC
c/o BET BOOKS
One BET Plaza
1900 W Place NE
Washington, D.C. 20018-1211

First Printing: June, 1999
10   9   8   7   6   5   4   3   2   1

Printed in the United States of America

ACKNOWLEDGEMENTS

I want to thank the countless fans who have continually been supportive of me over the years, buying the books, telling their friends, and buying more books! I hope to continue to be able to entertain, inform, and make you smile for many years to come. To my family and my friends, who always keep me grounded. To all the Arabesque authors new and old I have had the pleasure of meeting, e-mailing, and sharing with. Continued success to you all. To my editor, Karen Thomas, who allowed me to try something new, for having faith that I could pull it off. Thank you! And most of all, to God, who continues to shower me with daily blessings!

DEDICATION

For Robert
for always . . .

MAXINE

ONE

My Forever Came Today

I chased sleep all last night, doing my own version of the dead man's float on land. Not moving, stifling my sobs, I dared not toss or turn though my heart raced and my brain churned.

Taylor, my man, my lover's, gentle, enflaming touch unnerved me instead of igniting my heart. He wanted to make love to me—inside out. I knew what he needed, what he wanted, but something inside me shut down. And I was scared. Scared of what it meant.

"Tell me what's wrong, Baby. Talk to me," he'd said when I mumbled some incoherent excuse about not feeling up to it. Never in our three year relationship could we keep our hands off each other, right from the very beginning. *Did he know I was lying?*

Even as still as I remained, as hard as I worked at keeping my treacherous thoughts sealed shut, commanding my heart to stop that thudding noise, Taylor still worried about me. "Max? What's wrong, Baby?" He stroked my hair. "Want me to get you something?" He began to massage my neck, my back, releasing the knots of tension. That's the way he was—sensitive and in tune with my needs, my feelings. He always listened to me, *really* listened, and that made all the difference in the world. Taylor was always more than my man. He was my friend.

From the day we met, it was as if we'd known each other all our lives. There was an easiness about Taylor that just made it so simple to open up to him and not to be afraid of what he might see. From the beginning it drew me to him like a magnet—the need to be cared about totally and completely without having to fight for it.

I wanted to turn into his arms last night, pour out my heart and my darkest fears, bury them in the strength and security of his embrace, but for the first time in the three glorious years that we'd been together I couldn't. So I did the first thing that came to my mind, did something I'd sworn I'd never do. I lied. I lied to keep from hurting him with the truth.

"Mmm. Nothin', Babe, really. Just thinking about some things at work. Sorry if I'm keepin' you up." I eased out of the bed, nude as usual—Taylor liked that—and slipped on the short, peach silk robe that I kept at the foot of the four–poster bed. "Maybe some warm milk would help." I leaned down and kissed his temple, there on that salt and pepper spot that I sometimes teased him about but secretly thought only added to his ruggedly handsome looks.

"I'll sit with you," he mumbled, his voice a cross between Isaac Hayes's seductive timbre and tires running over gravel. That made me smile.

"Don't even think about it, Ty. Go back to sleep, Babe."

Still emotionally rattled, I tiptoed out of the room, walked down the short hallway, and peeked in at the par-tially open bedroom door. Something inside of me filled, just as it always did whenever I looked at my son, hunched up like a lump of sugar beneath his Spiderman sheets. *My blessing.*

I stood for a moment in the doorway, watching Jamel breathe in and out and the battlefield of action heroes spread out across the sheets, some having fallen onto the navy blue–carpeted floor.

My throat clenched. Three years ago, with one simple phone call, one sentence, this all could be so different— this life I had worked to build—but that was then.

Inhaling my reality, I let it settle in the unlit place inside myself and headed downstairs to think.

That was nearly four hours and three cups of coffee ago. Everything was still out of focus. The only thing that was a bit clear was the view of the Golden Gate Bridge that was slowly materializing beyond my little window on the world.

The beacons of sun streaming into the kitchen window were warm as always for eight A.M., even if they were filtered by the everpresent fog that hung over San Francisco like gauze drapes used to keep mosquitoes out. Music, coming from the little clock radio on the sink, slow and bluesy— the kind that slips through your pores and seeps into your soul—floated around the squared–off yellow room, bringing its own brand of "just sit back and relax." But I couldn't.

Above me, from upstairs, I heard the rush of the shower pounding against the ecru–colored tiles, and knew that Taylor was up. Any minute, like clockwork, Jamel would come bounding down the stairs, sleep still stuck in his inky black eyes, eyes just like his father's, wanting his bowl of Frosted Flakes with no milk.

For all intents and purposes it was a day just like any other, except for the boulder of truth that sat on my chest. There was no way I could put off telling Taylor much longer.

How many times in the past twenty-four hours had I wished that my old homegirl Val hadn't called from New York—that she hadn't mentioned Quinten Parker's name again, hadn't made me remember what I'd struggled these past years to forget?

For a fleeting moment, when she told me that Nikita was dead, there was that dark, ugly instant when I was almost relieved, vindicated somehow. From the day Quinn met Nikita Harrell, our relationship shifted. I'd known Quinten Parker nearly my entire life. His twin sister, Lacy, was my best friend, before she was killed. There was a bond between Quinn and me, one that I'd fantasized about and thought could never be broken.

We came from the same roots, talked the same language. I took the unspoken relationship between us as an inevitable given. Then Nikita walked into his life—the girl from the right side of the tracks, the last person I, or anyone, ever imagined Quinten Parker falling for—and my dreams of a lifetime with Quinn fell to pieces. Nikita Harrell rudely awakened me.

But then, as Val and I hung up, being human stepped in, and that unexplainable love harbored in my heart for Quinn since I was six-years-old suddenly roared to life, like dry wood stacked too close to the flame. And all that other stuff didn't matter. I hurt for him, felt his pain as surely as if it were my own—just as I'd always done. When—when—would he finally find his peace, some happiness? Everything—everyone—he'd ever loved was taken from him, one by one. And I was no better than the fates that dealt Quinn an unwinable hand. I wrapped both of mine around my mug.

The coffee was cold now, but I drank it anyway, rewinding last night in my head. I should have made love with Taylor. I should have let him into my soul to push away the images of Quinn that were resurrected, wash away the doubts that began to form around the edges of my heart.

Quinn. Q. His face loomed in front of me. Those long, silky dreads that must be almost to his waist by now. Those mesmerizing eyes, the wicked, dimpled smile, and thrill—your fingers that could stroke the blacks and whites of a keyboard and steal your soul. Oh, yeah, I remembered. I remembered the dreams we shared, the laughter, the pain, the bed—

"You never came back upstairs last night," Taylor said, standing in the archway of the kitchen, catching me completely off guard. *When did the shower go off?*

I looked up at him and tried to smile. Momentarily he paused, his long body held in that just to the side angle that gave the impression he didn't have a care in the world. One of the things that had attracted me to Taylor Collins was his total air of casualness.

"I know. I, uh didn't want to keep you up, and I knew I wouldn't be able to get back to sleep."

He eased into the kitchen and pulled out a chair from beneath the table and straddled it, bracing his arms across the rounded top. He rested his chin on his forearms and caressed my cheek with a stroke of his finger. "You wanna tell me what's really bothering you, Max? Or are you going to keep running the line about the job?"

"It's not a line. It's—"

"Don't lie to me, Baby. I know you, remember? Something's bothering you, and has been from the moment you walked in the door last night. And I know good and damned well it's not the job. You could run that travel agency of yours with your eyes closed." He looked at me for a long moment, his warm brown eyes waiting, probing.

"Mommy, I'm hungry," Jamel announced the instant his toes crossed the threshold of the kitchen. I was sure Taylor heard my sigh of relief.

"Mornin', Sweetie," I cooed, giving him a sweeping hug.

"Hey, Shortstop," Taylor said, rubbing his big hands across Jamel's head, much to his delight.

"Hi, Daddy." He giggled.

I got up from my perch and took the box of Frosted Flakes from the cabinet and filled a bowl for Jamel.

"We'll talk tonight, Max," Taylor said, making sure I didn't miss the no—nonsense tone in his voice. He stood, slid his arm around my waist, and pulled me close. "Whatever it is, we'll work it out. We always do."

He dipped his head and took a long, lazy kiss, then eased back, his eyes smoky with desire. I knew that look.

"Okay?"

All I could do was nod my head as he turned toward Jamel.

"See ya later, Slugger." He snatched Jamel up and gave him a tight squeeze. "Love you, buddy."

"Love you, too."

Taylor put him down and walked out.

The self—imposed noose of avoidance by silence grew taut around my neck. And I knew the longer I dodged the inevitable the tighter it would become.

After the usual ritual of getting Jamel ready for day care, doing a quick straightening up of our two—story town house, I found myself alone with my thoughts and my decision—one that I couldn't put off much longer. "Nikita's funeral is in two days, Max," Val had said. "I know it's hard, and probably asking too much, but you should be there. You and Quinn ... well ... there's history between you two. I think he needs you, Girl, but he'd never say that."

She was right. Quinn never would say he needed anyone. He was used to doing everything on his own, from the time he was sixteen, a man since he was a boy. His self—assurance and confident swagger only camouflaged the tenderness that rested in his spirit, but it was the lure of inaccessibility that always intrigued me, drawing me to him like a moth to a flame—the desire that was a part of me, to reach him, heal him. Oh, yes. I knew him.

But no matter what my decision, there was still my business to run and Jamel to raise. Slipping on my suit jacket, I headed for the door.

As usual, the morning rush hour traffic was a monster. Front ends kissed rear ends for miles, at least as far as you could see through the haze. After a while, though, you get used to it. So, rather than give myself a headache by chiming in with the other horn blowers, I turned up the volume on the radio, eased back a little in the seat, and listened to some cool jazz. My girl Phyllis Hyman was working one of her songs, and I sang right along with her. In some other life I just knew I was a singer.

Peeking across the lane to my left, one of those suit and tie-wearing brothers was having a heated argument on his cell phone. I immediately felt sorry for the poor soul on the other end. Even from my vantage point I could see the veins popping out on his forehead. To my right, a woman with four kids in her backseat appeared to be trying desperately to keep them from jumping out of the windows.

I wasn't sure which was worse, creeping along to work at a snail's pace or being trapped underground on a New York subway, engulfed by the pungent odors of the city and the cloying scents of every designer perfume under the sun. Even so, there were days when I actually missed that.

Picking up stakes from New York and moving to San Francisco was a hard decision. My entire life, everything and everyone that was familiar, I left behind. But five years ago, it was the only choice to be made. The need to start over, to break away from the ties that bound, were more powerful than the desire to stay. The only problem was that the cord wasn't broken.

Not too longer after my arrival, just when I was getting

my head together and my business off the ground, letting my spirit mend, Quinn arrived. At the time, I thought it was for good, that the day I'd longed for finally arrived. We spent two years together, moving from the tentative stages of friends to lovers. Foolishly, I believed that away from New York, away from the pain and the relationships of the past, he and I could really build a life together. I was wrong.

Quinn had ties, too, ties more potent than anything I could bind him with. Somewhere, buried deep inside, there was a part of me that knew he'd go back. Back to New York. Back to Nikita. I just didn't want to believe it.

Humph. Quinn and Nikita. Ms. Uptown Girl. But hey, got to give her credit, she loved him. I suppose. The problem was, so did I at the time. It took letting go and letting Taylor into my life to finally find my piece of the happiness pie. Now, with one phone call, it felt as if my whole world were being turned upside down again. *No dessert for you.*

My eyes began to burn, and it had nothing to do with the smog. How was I going to explain to Taylor that I needed to go back to New York to be with Quinn? Better yet, how was I going to face Quinn for the first time in three years and not tell him about his son?

"Didn't think I'd ever make it," I said, breezing into the office on a gust of hot air an hour later. I tossed my purse on top of my always overloaded desk and flopped down in the cushioned chair.

Marva, my business partner and dear friend, glanced up from her computer screen and grinned as if everything was just lovely.

"Max, you say that at least once a week." She kept clicking the keys. "You know you don't have to be here every day. It's a trek for you. I can handle things."

I looked at her bowed brunette head for a moment, and

knew she was right. But the fact of the matter was, as much as I might fuss and cuss about the distance, the traffic, and the smog, I loved it all, and I loved my business. This was mine—*my* dream—and I guess I just needed to see it every day to make sure it *wasn't* a dream.

"Did you talk with Taylor yet?" she asked over her rapid–fire typing.

I could hear the note of hesitancy, the slight hitch in her voice. She stared right at me yesterday when Val called, when that bottom–dropped–out–of–my world look came across my face. At first she thought something happened to Jamel or Taylor, and she almost freaked out until I finally got myself together enough to explain about Val's call.

Marva was there for me with a hug and a smile when Quinn arrived in Frisco. She let me use her shoulder when he left and went back to Nikita. And no one was happier for me than Marva when Taylor came into my life. "You deserve to be happy, Girl," she'd said. "Go for it."

I pressed the power button on my computer and tried to act as if I didn't hear—"Did you talk with Taylor?"—the million dollar question.

"Don't act like you didn't hear me, Maxine Sherman." She spun her chair until we were eyeball to eyeball, crossed her arms beneath her ample breasts, and waited. I could almost see her counting off the seconds in her head. "Well?" she snapped, and I jumped.

"No. I didn't talk to Taylor last night." I tried to sound defiant. She wasn't impressed.

Her thick brows bunched together. "Max, when are you planning on talking to him—at the airport? Girl, I don't believe you."

"I'm glad you think it's so damned easy, Marva. News flash—it's not." I rolled my eyes as hard as I could, hoping she'd get the message that I was really ticked off with her.

"I know it's not easy. Life isn't easy. But it's not going

to get better by putting it off. Unless you've changed your mind and decided not to go."

Her dark blue eyes zeroed in on my face and stayed there. I was the first to look away.

Blowing out a long breath of frustration, I got up and began to pace. Pacing always seemed to help. Or at least it used to.

"Marva, I swear I've been up half the night trying to find a way to tell Taylor that I need to go to New York. I couldn't."

"Why? Taylor is one of the most understanding men I've ever met—"

"Being understanding is one thing, Marva. Accepting that—one—you're raising the son of the man your woman was in love with as your own, and—two—she's making plans to be by his side in his time of need, is a lot for *any* man to handle. I don't care how understanding he is," I shot back, needing to sound annoyed to justify my own lack of assertiveness.

"You know better than that, Max. Taylor loves you, and he loves Jamel. He knew the deal when he met you, and it didn't stop him. Have a little trust in him."

Trust. I swallowed hard, tossing the ominous word around in my head. I raised my gaze to meet hers. "It's not Taylor I don't trust. It's me." Well, you could have heard a pin drop on the carpet.

Marva gave me "the look"—you know, the one your mother would flash when you were out of order, and you snapped to attention? I almost felt like bowing my head and shuffling my feet in contrition.

"I know you're going to explain." Her head angled to an even forty–five degrees.

I tried to dodge what I knew was coming next by, pacing faster.

"Max . . . please don't tell me—"

Fancy footwork be damned. I came to a full, screeching

stop. "Tell you what? That I think I still have unresolved feelings for Quinn? That I see his face every time I look at *our* son?" I picked up my pace again. "That when I got the phone call from Val, the first thing I felt was *glad* that Nikita was out of his life? That when I got in bed last night with the man who has always loved me from the bottom of his soul I didn't want him to touch me because I remembered Quinn's hands on my body? Is that what you *don't* want me to tell you?"

I was fuming now, ready for a fight, and Marva was the most likely opponent, if for no other reason than because she was there. I was pissed, angry, confused—with myself—and I had to take it out on somebody. I knew I sounded as if I'd just gone around the bend. My voice had reached a borderline pitch that makes the hair on your arms begin to tingle. I couldn't help it, not with my heart racing as if I'd been running a marathon.

All of a sudden I felt Marva's arm around my shoulder, pulling me close, halting my steps, and muttering all those comforting things you say to someone whose edges are frayed.

"Come on, hon. Sit down and catch your breath."

She ushered me to my chair, helping me into it like she thought I might fall, or something. I loved her for what she was doing, but in a momentary state of clarity I felt like an idiot.

Marva crossed the office, which wasn't much larger than your average classroom, locked the door, and hung the CLOSED sign in the window. She rolled her chair across the floor until our knees bumped. She took my hands and kneaded them between her long, soft fingers.

I sniffed and looked down at our entwined hands, hers so pale with pink undertones, and mine the color of Hershey chocolate. What a pair we made. But you couldn't tell *us* we weren't sisters. Marva Torino had soul to the bone. A true sistah in the wrong body. In the years Marva and I worked together at the agency we'd become solid friends. I shared things with Marva that I never shared with anyone—not with Val, not Lacy, not even Taylor. I never imagined I could be friends with a white girl—especially one like Marva, who came from money and privilege, me being raised in the heart of struggle and hopelessness—but something between us clicked from the beginning, and the color thing didn't matter. She was my friend. One who didn't pull any punches and would stand toe–to–toe with me no matter how far back into the neighborhood I went, and give it right back to me.

Marva was privy to my intense but abbreviated romance with Quinn, the pain I felt when he left me. She was the first person I told about the baby I was carrying. I confided in her about my doubts about getting involved with Taylor, especially under the circumstances. I trusted her and her judgment. And our sharing was never one–sided. Marva always found a way to weave in a life lesson for me from snippets of her decade–old romance and marriage to Brent.

"If I had left it up to my parents and my friends, my relationship with Brent would have been doomed," she once told me. "I came from a world of private schools, lawns that needed a team of mowers, high society, and old British money. Brent's parents were "common," "beneath me," "an embarrassment," "laborers." My parents threatened to disown me if I married him.

"But you know what, Maxine? I didn't give a damn. Still don't." She chuckled wickedly. "Brent made my heart and my body sing. He opened up the real world to me, and he loved me with every ounce of his being. I'd never had that before, and I can only hope that everyone has a glimmer of what he and I share. So I went against them—my parents, my friends, tradition. And I never looked back or regretted one minute. Sometimes in life, Maxine, we have to make hard choices, choices that can hurt. But we also have to be willing to deal with the consequences of our choices. If we can do that, then it's half the battle.''

That conversation and countless others like it had sustained me on many a troubled night, and I sure needed her uncanny wisdom right about now.

"Tell me what's going on in your head, Max," she said, cutting into my thoughts.

I let out a breath, laden with doubt. "I . . . don't know what to do, Marva. I want to see Quinn. Maybe too much. And it's scaring me. It scares me to think about what may happen when I get to New York."

"What do you think will happen, Max? What are you afraid of?"

I bit down on my lip for a moment, knowing that once I said the words out loud, the words that danced around in my head they'd become real, and I couldn't take them back. I paused, stood up, and sat back down.

"I'm . . . afraid I'll realize I never stopped loving Quinn, and screw up everything I have with Taylor," I said in a torrent of words and raw emotion. "Afraid that what I've built with Taylor is all a carefully constructed illusion. That it isn't real, only a substitute for what I think I lost."

She was quiet for a moment. "I see. And what about Jamel? Can you face Quinn and not tell him about his son? And when you do, what then?"

The noose around my neck tightened a bit more. I struggled for air. "Three years, Marva. Three years since he left and went back to New York." I swallowed and looked over her head, focusing on the rack of travel brochures on the other side of the room. "And most days I hardly think about what might have been. But then there are those days when I think how cruel it is to deprive Quinn of the knowledge of his son. Yet, Taylor is the only father Jamel has ever known. How right is that?"

"Why didn't you ever tell Quinn? It's not as if you didn't have the opportunity."

"When I found out I was pregnant, Quinn had been back in New York and with Nikita for almost three months—shortly before you started working here. They were a week away from getting married. I didn't want him coming back to me just because I was pregnant. That's the oldest trick in the book. I wanted him back only if he loved me, and I didn't believe he did. Not really. Not the kind of love I needed. And then Taylor walked through that door right over there, into my life and my heart, and made all the hurt go away. He made me believe in myself again."

"But how do you feel about Taylor, Maxine, really feel? Right now—today."

I looked at her then, right in her midnight–blue eyes. "I love him."

"And Quinn?"

"I don't know."

"Then you need to go to New York. For your sake, Taylor's, and Jamel's. You're never going to have peace until you finally face Quinn and either put closure to these feelings you have—"

"Or see if what I already have with Taylor is all I need."

"Yes. My sentiments exactly."

We didn't talk about my "situation" any more for the balance of the morning. That's just the way Marva was. Once she'd said what was on her mind, that was it.

Unfortunately, that didn't mean it was off mine. Whenever there was a lull in the day's activity, after I'd finished booking the trip of a lifetime for yet another customer, my "situation" would tiptoe up behind me and tap me on the shoulder. *Hey, don't forget me,* it would whisper in my ear. I wanted to slap it away like an annoying fly, but I couldn't. It just settled back down and waited for the next opportunity to sneak up on me again.

"I'm going to take a break for lunch," Marva announced. "I have some errands to run. You want to come?"

"No. Go ahead."

"Want me to bring you anything?"

"No. I'll probably go out when you get back."

"Okay. See you in about an hour."

I tried to concentrate on surfing the Internet to see what kind of sales some of the other travel agencies were offering when the bell chimed over the door. I looked up and a thirtyish, good-looking man walked in. He was tall, about Taylor's height, maybe six-two or so. He was dressed casually in one of those nylon designer jogging suits, looking ready to hang out for a minute. His dark brown skin glistened with a slight sheen of perspiration. He was pleasant enough to look at—more than once—which I did, and I caught a glint of light bouncing off the third finger of his left hand.

"Hi. How can I help you?"

He walked farther into the office, cautious, and looked around as if trying to determine if we were alone. He shoved his hands into the pockets of his electric blue windbreaker. My antennae went up, and I instantly wished I'd taken Marva up on her offer to go to lunch. I stood—ready for anything, bumping the back of my knees against the chair, my hand near the phone.

He cleared his throat. "I hope so." He gave me a shy smile. "I, uh wanted to book a flight to Chicago."

Chicago. I almost said it out loud in relief. My pulse slowed down just a notch. "Of course. Why don't you have a seat and tell me your plans?" I indicated the chair next to my desk.

He eased into the chair, stretching his long legs out in front of him.

"When were you planning to leave?"

"Day after tomorrow."

"Short notice." I started to give him my standard speech about the advantages of booking well in advance, but something told me that this trip was a last minute decision, that stopping in was on impulse. His next comment confirmed my conclusion.

"I've debated about going for almost a month."

"A month? Why did you wait so long?"

He shrugged slightly. "Wasn't sure if it was the best thing to do."

"Book early, or take the trip?" I teased, which got a chuckle out of him. I kept typing.

"Take the trip."

My right eyebrow arched in question. "Oh. So what made you finally decide to go ahead with it?"

"Funny thing is, I'm still not sure."

At that point I didn't know whether to be curious or annoyed. I hoped he didn't think he was going to get a refund if he changed his mind.

"Is there a problem?"

He didn't answer.

"You are aware that this ticket is non–refundable?"

"Yes. I know." He stood up, walked across the room to the rack of brochures, and picked up one detailing the wonders of Hawaii. "Went here on my honeymoon," he said, almost to himself.

I watched him for a moment threading along the cross-roads of decision, and then I saw something in his eyes, a momentary flicker as if he'd seen something pleasant, and he smiled again. Just a little.

"I hear it's beautiful."

"More like heaven on earth," he said.

His body seemed to relax and let go, then, as if the strain of carrying a burden had finally been removed, the tension flowed from him on a tide of expelled air, leaving him open and receptive. All of a sudden I realized he wasn't out to give me a hard time, but was really battling with his decision about the trip.

"Will your wife need a ticket as well?"

His head snapped in my direction, as if realizing he wasn't alone.

"No. She doesn't like to fly."

"Is it business or pleasure?"

He inhaled deeply, his chest expanding, then blew out a long breath. "It's a college reunion."

I smiled, wondering what that was like. I'd never gone any further than business school, to get my agency certificate. Couldn't see any college reunions in my future.

"That sounds like fun. How many years has it been?"

"Ten." He turned toward me.

"I'd think you'd want to go. A lot happens to people in ten years. You can joke about folks who've gone bald, gotten pot bellies and wound up with the wrong wives." I laughed lightly at the images.

His dark eyes suddenly locked with mine, and my heart knocked. *What had I said?*

"That's part of the problem," he said out of nowhere.

"I'm not sure I understand."

"Neither do I."

He was quiet for a while as he absently fingered the brochures, looking around the office, but not really seeing. I thought that would be all he'd reveal. But then, like a young thief eager to make a confession, he let the words pour out of him.

"I just know that going back may resurrect some things that are best left buried."

My "situation" tapped me on the shoulder again. "Then . . . why go?"

"That's what I've asked myself these past weeks. But if I don't go, too many questions will be left unanswered. I'll never really know if I made the right decision."

"Made the right decision—you mean about your job, where you decided to live . . . ?"

Slowly he shook his head. "No. About the woman I chose to marry."

"Oh," was all I could summon in response. His confession surprised me in its bold honesty and its reflection of my life, and something inside of me needed to know if there was a solution to my own quandary. Maybe he had it, this stranger.

I looked at him for a moment. His face was gone. In its place was my own, staring back at me, waiting. In the blink of an eye what began as a benign conversation suddenly took a serious twist. What could I say to him, to this man who felt the need to share a part of himself with a total stranger, to one who wouldn't be judgmental? Perhaps that's what made it easy.

"I think I understand," slipped across my lips.

"You do?" He sounded mystified, and absently sat down opposite me.

I nodded, thoughtful. "I'm sort of at a crossroads myself. And have probably asked the same questions as you." I leaned forward on the desk and clasped my hands, staring at them for a moment. I looked at him, and our gazes connected in that inexplicable split second when you realize that a chance meeting has the potential to change your future.

He fingered his wedding band.

"How long?" I asked, pointing to the ring.

"Three years."

"Any kids?"

"Yeah." He grinned. "A little girl."

"That's nice. Kids make things worthwhile."

"Yeah. But sometimes they're good camouflage for what you don't want to see or deal with."

Was Jamel camouflage for me? Was I using my son as a shield, to keep from dealing with the truth? Was I using him to convince myself that as long as he was happy, cared for, and loved, everything was as it seemed—the picture of a perfect nuclear family—that Jamel didn't represent

my tie to the past with Quinn and my road to the future
with Taylor? I shook off the notion.

"What about you? Any kids?"

I nodded. "A little boy, Jamel."

"Hmm." He looked away, seemingly lost in thought.

"Is this—person—you think you should have married
going to be at the reunion?"

"Yes. She's the one who sent me the invitation. Humph.
I didn't know she'd kept up with me," he added in a
faraway voice.

"Oh." Did Quinn know that I'd kept up with him over
the years through Val? That I knew about the success of
the foundation he'd started in his sister Lacy's memory,
or that I listened to his CD in the privacy of my car? That
I knew he was working on another book, and he and Nikita
had often visited Shug's Fish Fry in Harlem on Friday
nights? Yeah, I knew. It was as though by catching snippets
of his life I could vicariously remain a part of it. Although
the tidbits of news were often few and far between, they
filled some of the spaces. Sometimes.

"Do you think the trip to Chicago is going to change
things between you and your wife?" I knew what I was
really asking. I was asking him about *me,* my life, and I
needed to hear the answer from someone who stood to
lose everything. As I did.

"I'm sure it will. One way or the other. I think that's
what scares me—the fact that my marriage will be tested,
my vows held up for inspection." He stood. "But if I don't
go, I'll never have the answers." He looked directly into
my eyes. "Will I?"

I felt as if I held the future of this stranger's life in my
hand. With one word I could decide his fate—and more
importantly, my own as well.

"No. You won't. You never will. And until you do, you'll
always ask yourself what if? Nothing will ever be whole."
Then all at once everything crystallized for me. I knew I

must take the chance. Go against the odds, and deal with the consequences. It would never be fair to Taylor for me to be unsure, be with him as a second choice. I needed to clear the path behind me, so that I could move forward with Ty—no obstacles, no looking back.

He smiled, almost in thanks, I thought.

"Then I guess I'd better book that ticket. Round trip."

As I keyed in the last of the reservation information, I suddenly realized that he sounded so sure, so certain that what he had at home would be waiting for him when he returned. I prayed the same would be true for me. I had to believe that it would.

TWO

Now Comes the Hard Part

As I stuck my key in the lock of my town house several hours later and stepped inside, my heart thumped, and that funny dipping feeling took hold of my stomach.

"Mommy!" Jamel squealed, and he came barreling toward me as if he'd been shot from a cannon, right up into my arms, just as he did every evening.

He wrapped his little legs around my waist and his arms around my neck. I smothered his face with kisses until he was giddy with laughter. My heart filled.

"Did you bring me sumfin?"

"Yes." I kissed his cheek. "A lot of love."

He giggled. "Where?"

"In my purse, of course."

I dropped my purse on the hall table and carried him down the short foyer, heading in the direction of the scent of grilled salmon coming from the kitchen. *Yeah, Ty was working his magic.* The thought made me smile.

"Hi, Babe," I said to his back while he continued to cut up fixings for a side salad.

I put Jamel down and eased up behind Taylor, sliding my arms around his waist, pressing my head against the expanse of his back. Mmm, he smelled good. If only I could wrap myself up in his essence.

"Hi, yourself."

He turned from the sink, grabbed a dishtowel to dry his hands, and pulled me full against him. We fit, every dip, every curve. Perfect.

I raised my head, looking up at him while he lowered his, brushing soft lips teasingly across mine. A shudder spread through me, like water being skimmed with a stone, just as it had from the moment we met.

Taylor's body was sculpted from dedicated hours at the gym. Muscles rippled beneath his shirt, and I never grew tired of running my hands over him. I remember when he first walked into the door of the travel agency—all I could think was, *Oh my God.* He had this—this—walk that defied explanation, smooth like a long lazy panther with a touch of urban assuredness—casual but raw. His skin reminded me of warm brandy, and there was a faint shadow of a beard stroking his strong chin, with a dimple dead center that gave him a rugged, but boyish look. And yet it wasn't so much the good looks, the drop–dead body, arrogant swagger, or Isaac Hayes voice that caught and held me. It was the soft center, the quiet strength that hovered just beneath the surface that intoxicated me.

"We're going to put Jamel to bed early so we can spend some time together," he said against my mouth.

"I like the sound of that."

"If I had my way, I'd like to spend that time right now," he said from deep in his throat, and I felt the urgency of his need press against me. "You feel good to me, Max."

His fingers played along the sensitive cord of my spine, sending shock waves down the length of my body. I felt weak with need, and then laced with guilt as images of Quinn bloomed before me like an erupting volcano.

Ty stepped back. "What is it, Maxine? Why is it when I touch you lately, you freeze up on me?"

I turned away to hide the truth. "That's not true, and you know it."

"Do I?" He tossed the dishtowel onto the countertop and turned away. "I'm going up to take a shower," he said more to the room than to me, then stormed out.

I shut my eyes and leaned against the counter. Oh, God, I didn't want to hurt him. Not Ty. I'd heard the pain in his voice. I did that. What was I doing? What was wrong with me? Maybe it was best that I didn't go. Leave well enough alone. Just the thought of the trip was putting a strain on our relationship.

But then the conversation I'd had with the man at the agency filtered through my thoughts, and I understood that if I didn't go and put these feelings to rest they would always haunt me, and float like ghosts between me and Ty. *What if?*

The scent of Taylor suddenly wrapped around me—conjured from my memory, I thought—until I opened my eyes. For an instant it felt as if my heart suddenly stopped beating.

Taylor was standing in front of me holding my airline tickets in his hand.

A rush of heat ignited in the pit of my stomach and jettisoned to my head, which began to pound. *Dear Lord, not like this.*

"Seems Jamel was looking for a treat in your bag and found these."

He held them toward me, like a prosecutor displaying to the jury the final piece of evidence to convict the defendant.

"Planning to go to New York without saying anything, Max?"

His voice, the low rumble of thunder before the stroke of lightning, vibrated in my chest. His dark eyes narrowed. What I saw in them wasn't anger, but betrayal. I stood accused. *Guilty as charged.*

I reached out to him and he took an almost imperceptible step back. My insides quivered.

"Ty . . . I was going to tell you—"

"When, Maxine?"

"Tonight."

He tossed his head back and barked out a one–note laugh. "Tonight. How convenient." He took a step closer. "What's in New York, Max? Huh?"

His eyes cinched making his expression hard.

"What could possibly be in New York that you wouldn't tell me about until you were ready to walk out the door?"

"Ty, if you'll just listen, I'll explain," I tossed back with a touch of bravado, trying to stall for a few seconds to clear my head.

"I'm listening, Maxine. So tell me, what's in New York?"

He leaned against the refrigerator and crossed his arms, the damning tickets dangling from his fingertips.

I began to pace. "Val—my friend from New York—"

"I know who Val is."

I cleared my throat. "She called and told me that . . . Quinn's wife, Nikita, was killed in a car accident. The . . . funeral is day after tomorrow."

For an instant there was a flash of shock in his eyes mixed with compassion. His stiff expression momentarily relaxed. His gaze met mine.

"I'm sorry to hear that, Max, but what does that have to do with you?"

"We were . . . he's Jamel's . . ." I blew out a breath. I was making a real mess out of this. "I should be there, Ty. He was someone important to me . . . once. He's had so many tragedies in his life, Ty," I said as the pain welled inside me—with the memories of how he'd taken care of his sister Lacy when their mother walked out on them, and then losing Lacy in that horrid shoot–out—hoping I could find the words to make him understand. "I need to be there . . . as a friend."

"You sure that's all, Max—a *friend*?"

I planted my hands on my hips. "What are you trying to say?" I asked, guilt toughening my voice, while my insides shook.

"I'm not *trying* to say anything. I *said* it. If it's just about you being a *friend*, then why all the cloak and dagger? Why the cold shoulder toward me?"

The catch in his voice was unmistakable, even as he stood in front of me challenging, demanding. Beneath the ironclad exterior, he cradled his hurt and feelings about breach of trust.

My throat tightened. "Ty, I—"

"It makes me think you're hiding something, you know. Like maybe you still have feelings for him. That you couldn't tell me because you feel guilty. Is that the real deal, Maxine? Because if it is, I want to know. Now."

A jumble of emotions and perfect–for–the–circumstances answers volleyed for position. I know he claimed to want the truth, but I couldn't believe that he really did. And how could I explain to him the maelstrom of confusion that was waging war inside me?

"Hey. You don't even have to say anything. Your silence is answer enough."

He handed me the tickets, walked out of the kitchen and through the front door, its dull thud a perfect epitaph to the end of my day.

Jamel walked into the kitchen, his thumb stuck in his mouth, eyes downcast. "Where Daddy go?"

I bent down and scooped him up, anchoring him on my hip. "Daddy just went for a walk," I said, hoping it was true. I kissed his forehead.

"I'm hungry," he mumbled over his thumb, resting his head on my shoulder.

I looked around, dinner all but forgotten, the remnants of the half–made salad still in the sink. The casserole dish filled with grilled salmon on its bed of yellow rice and zucchini sat on the kitchen counter. Signs of Taylor's caring touch were everywhere—the sunshine yellow walls he'd recently painted, the new cabinets he'd put in on his free weekends, the stereo system he'd replaced when mine hit its last note. Even Jamel, who was always bathed and cared for when I arrived home from work.

I held Jamel a bit tighter. Taylor was a good man, better than good. There was nothing too big or too small around the house for him to deal with, no problem too trivial for him to listen to. I never had to worry about where he was at night because he was always home, with me and Jamel.

"I want to make a life for us, Maxine," he'd said several months after we'd met, even as my belly grew fuller with Quinn's child.

"But, Ty, what about the baby? I know it's going to be hard to—"

"I can make you happy, Maxine. You and the baby. I love you, and I'm going to love the child you're carrying just like my own. It doesn't matter as long as we're together," he'd said running his hand along my cheek. "Give me a chance, Max. Give us a chance."

When I'd looked into his eyes, the depth of love and sincerity radiated from them and entered my soul. In that moment I decided to give in to my emotions, let Taylor enter my heart and allow his love to fill me. Stop fighting what seemed our destiny. And every day that he'd been in my life was a blessing. No woman could ask for more from a man. Taylor exceeded all of his promises to me and to Jamel.

Yet, here I stood—alone—unable to tell this very same man that there was nothing and no one more important to me than him. Not even Quinten Parker. And the *why not* is what chilled me.

"Mommy, you cryin'?"

I blinked, then looked at my son. "No, sweetie," I said over a wobbly smile. "I just have something in my eye."

"I'm still hungry."

I sniffed. "Then let's get you something to eat."

After fixing Jamel's dinner and then settling him down for bed, I spent the next few hours alternating between jumping up to look out the window at every sound, and checking the phone to make sure it was working.

Every noise made me think it was Taylor returning home. He didn't.

And I thought I would go out of my mind with worry. By the time two A.M. rolled around, I was ready to start calling hospitals. I envisioned the worst.

From the day we moved in together, we'd never spent a night apart. Until now. I wanted to kick myself. Why couldn't I have simply told him what he needed to hear? Why did I let him walk out believing that there was any man more important to me than him?

I stretched out across the bed, right on top of the comforter, too exhausted to pull it back. Staring up at the ceiling, I knew the answer, and it terrified me.

At some point sleep snatched me, buffeting me around on clouds of confusion, indecision, and guilt.

In a fitful sleep, I kept coming back to a fork after a long walk down an empty road. One direction was filled with light, and sounds of laughter. In the other direction the path appeared to be filtered, as if I were seeing it through a thin mist, making it difficult for me to see anything except the figure of Quinn, who held his hand out to me. He promised me he'd love me always, for real this time. We could be a family. He needed his son.

I started to walk toward him. Then I heard Taylor's voice. "Don't go, Maxine. I need you, too. I love you. We are a family. Max!"

I looked toward Quinn, then Taylor.

"Max. Maxine."

My eyes flew open. For a moment the room was out of focus. When it cleared, Taylor was standing above me. It was morning. I sat up.

"Ty. Baby. I was worried. I'm sorry." I reached for him.

"I need to get ready for work." His tone was flat, emotionless.

He turned away and walked toward the closet. I got out of bed and followed him.

"Ty." I touched his back and felt him flinch beneath my fingertips as if my touch offended him. My stomach dipped and then settled, even as my heart raced with dread. "Where were you all night?"

"Around. Driving. Sitting. Thinking."

The words, thrown at me like darts, pierced the first layer of my spirit.

He took out his navy blue suit, and a stark white shirt. *He's always looked good in that outfit,* I thought abstractly, trying to grab hold of something, anything familiar, to settle the shifting beneath my feet and between Taylor and I.

"We need to talk, Ty."

"Yeah. Just not now. I'm tired and I'm late." He turned away, left the room, and slammed the bathroom door behind him.

For several moments I stared at the closed door, shut in my face, locking me out. Uncertainty and fear built steadily like a campfire within me, the flames fed by the winds of doubt.

Taylor never closed me out. Until now. Talking, sharing, had been the cornerstone of our relationship, of who we were, what kept it healthy, growing, alive. Without that cornerstone, it was only a matter of time before our foundation began to crumble, and everything with it.

Since the beginning, I instinctively knew I could count

on Taylor, his ability to anchor me, weather the storm—the assurance that no matter what we were in this relationship together, kept me grounded, secure. Now I faced a Taylor I did not know. This new reality danced without rhythm in my head.

Disoriented from our confrontation and groggy from a lack of a decent night's sleep, I made my way down the hall to wake Jamel for school.

"Where's Daddy?" Jamel mumbled, rubbing his eyes.

My chest heaved. "He's getting dressed for work, Sweetie. Come on. You need to get ready for school."

"I'm hungry."

"What else is new?" I teased, relishing the one thing that was familiar. It seemed as if my life was spinning out of sync, and the only thing holding me together was Jamel.

While I was preparing Jamel's bowl of Frosted Flakes, Taylor walked into the kitchen.

"Daddy!"

Jamel sprinted from his seat at the table and jumped into Taylor's arms.

"Hey, Buddy." He squeezed Jamel to him.

"You was gone," Jamel whined.

"I had some things to do, Buddy."

"I'm eating Frosted Flakes."

Taylor grinned, carried Jamel back to the table and deposited him in his seat.

"Make sure you eat it all so you can get big."

"Like you." He grinned and shoved a spoonful of cereal into his mouth.

Watching the two of them, so easy and comfortable with each other, my soul filled with so many emotions. How could I jeopardize this? Taylor, sensing my stare, looked up.

Sunlight streamed in through the kitchen window, resting, it seemed, on his wide shoulders. I saw his eyes then, looking dark and distant, the shadows of a sleepless night ringing them like poorly applied mascara.

My heart thumped in my chest.

"I'm late," was all he said to me before turning away and walking toward the front door.

"Taylor, wait."

I followed him, but it seemed he wasn't going to stop, as if he'd already dismissed me.

He put his hand on the door, stopped, and then turned toward me. For a moment he looked down, as if the words he was ready to speak had fallen and he was searching for them, needing to gather them up to make sense.

When he looked up at me, I knew I'd never felt such terror, such bottomless fear, that whatever was to come next would change our relationship forever.

He blew out a breath. "I've been doing a lot of thinking Max, all night. I never deluded myself into believing that I could ever replace Quinn, be Quinn in your life, in your heart, in your body. What I believe I brought to this relationship was something real, not that make–believe bull that you had happening with him.

"I love you, *and* Jamel—just like he's my own son. But he's not, and the first time that reality scared me was last night. It shook me, Max, that you'd take yourself up to New York, work out whatever you think you need to work out with this man, and then he'd come for his son. The boy I raised."

I saw his throat working up and down, as if he were trying to keep that knot of hurt from planting itself permanently there.

My eyes were burning, and I swore that my heart was being squeezed out of my chest. I wanted to run to him, wrap him in my arms, and make the past forty–eight hours disappear, make everything go back to the way it was. But I couldn't—just as Taylor told me when we'd first met.

"So." He blew out a long breath, raised his chin for a

moment, and gazed up at the ceiling as if he could no longer bear to look at me. "I decided that maybe it's best if you do go to New York, Max. Settle this thing once and for all, so that you can move on with your life." He jammed his hands into his pockets. "If there's one thing I've never done, it's stand in the way of what you wanted, and apparently going to New York to be with Quinn is it. No matter what that decision will do to us. You think about it, Maxine. Really think about it. I don't want you to go. I can't be any clearer than that. But the ball is in your court."

By the time I finally shook off the impact of his declaration, I heard his car pull out of the driveway.

He was gone. Out the door. And maybe out of my life.

Too many thoughts circled around me, like hungry buzzards waiting to pick apart an unlucky victim. Me.

What had I done? Better yet, what was I going to do? I was hard pressed to believe that Taylor would actually walk out on what we had simply because I elected to go to New York to be supportive of a friend during a difficult time.

But what if he did? Suppose he wasn't simply challenging me—what then?

No. He wouldn't do that. Not Taylor. We'd talk tonight when he came home. Really talk. I'd go to New York, come back, and everything would be as it was.

You're fooling yourself a voice whispered. *Things will never be as they were.*

"So, what are you going to do"? Marva asked me later that day after I'd told her about Taylor's ultimatum.

"I'm going. Just like I planned," I answered, trying to sound resolute. I propped my hip on the edge of her desk and crossed my arms.

"And risk what you have with Taylor? Is that what I'm hearing?"

"Taylor will understand when he calms down. And if he

doesn't, maybe what we have isn't all it's cracked up to be if he can't trust me.''

Marva let out a snide laugh. "If I remember correctly, it was *you* who said you didn't trust yourself.''

I rolled my eyes. "That was yesterday. I wasn't thinking clearly.''

"But you're thinking clearly now?" She flashed me "that look" again.

"I can handle this, Marva. I need to handle this. And Ty's just gonna have to give me the chance to do it.''

"Whatever you say, Maxine. And whatever it is you think you have to prove, I hope it's worth it.''

I got up from her desk, crossed the room with plenty of attitude, and plopped down in my chair. "If *I* remember correctly, you were the one who said I needed to go.''

"Listen, Max—bottom line, no one can tell you anything one way or the other. Only you know what's in your heart and mind, and what you're up against. Yes, you do need to settle this thing between you and Quinn. Yes, he does need to be told about his son. The question becomes, are you willing to deal with the consequences?''

I bit down on my lip—a bad habit I have when I'm wrestling with a problem. I tossed around what Marva said, and replayed Taylor's words of that morning. At some point I was going to have to come to terms with my feelings for Quinn, say all the things I never had the chance to say. And if not now, then when? But when I did, when I opened the door to the past, unlocked the secrets and spoke the words, nothing would be the same for any of us ever again.

I would be changed, and Quinn, Taylor, and Jamel. The fabric of our lives would become unraveled, and it would take everything that all of us had—what we shared—to put it together again. But what would the pattern of our lives really be? And could Taylor and I withstand the changes that my decision would evoke?

Taylor. I hadn't heard from him all day. My calls to his

office had gone unreturned. "He's in conference," was the first response. "He's out of the office," was next. "I left your messages," was said with just a taste of, "You're getting on my last nerve now," underlying the receptionist's voice. I had a good mind to call his partner CJ to find out where Taylor was, and what he was so involved in that he couldn't, or wouldn't, return my calls. I thought better of it. No point in getting CJ involved in our drama—although he probably knew, anyway.

Ty and CJ were thicker than the mob. The tie between them unbreakable. I knew CJ wasn't too crazy about me in the beginning. He felt I was bringing nothing but trouble and heartache into Taylor's life, and had no problem about telling me so.

"Don't mess with my man's head," he'd warned me as he carried a carton of Ty's CDs into the town house the day Ty moved in with me. "He really digs you, Maxine. Ty's a good brother, and I don't want to see him hurt. Not by you. Not by anybody."

His jaw clenched and I saw the muscles in his arms flex. His nut–brown face darkened ominously.

"I wouldn't hurt Taylor. I wouldn't," I swore, staring into his unflinching eyes. And at that moment, I knew CJ would have no problem making me a vague memory if I messed with his boy.

"Hey, listen, it's not about what you wouldn't do, Maxine. You got a lot of baggage comin' into this thing. Ty's not just takin' you on—but—"

He looked down at my rounded belly with an accusing look in his eyes. And all of a sudden I felt ashamed, almost guilty, and I wasn't sure why. There was nothing for me to be ashamed of. This baby, *my* baby, was conceived in love. Not some one–night stand.

". . . you know what I mean," he was saying.

"Yeah, I know exactly what you mean, Calvin," I snapped, ready for a throw–down. "But the bottom line is, this is between me and Taylor. You can have whatever opinion you want about me. That's your business. But when it's all said and done, it's about us loving each other and making a life together. Now you may not like me," I said, getting on a serious roll. "I can't worry about that. I'm not in this to win a popularity contest with you as the judge. The only person whose opinion matters, one way or the other, is Taylor. Period. End of story."

We stared each other down for a minute, and then all of a sudden his expression softened and he tossed his head back and laughed.

"You know something, Maxine Sherman—you're all right."

He strolled into the house and the topic never came up again. Over the ensuing months, CJ and I actually became good friends, close. We respected each other's boundaries and accepted the fact that we both loved Taylor.

It was CJ who took me to the hospital when I went into labor, and held my hand until Taylor arrived on a red–eye flight from Chicago. He stood as Jamel's godfather, and I bent his ear on many an occasion planning surprise parties for Ty's birthdays, or crazy anniversary ideas I'd come up with. And it was me he came to all love–struck and tongue–tied when he wanted to ask his longtime girlfriend, Tracy, to marry him.

"What if she says no?" he lamented.

"CJ, what if she says yes, fool? You know she will. That's what's scaring you."

He grinned and kissed me on the cheek. "That's why I dig you, Max. You don't pull any punches. So—you gonna come with me to pick out a ring, or what?"

Sure, I could call CJ, ask him what was going on with Taylor, but I didn't think I could stand to hear what I knew would be accusation and disappointment in his voice.

Besides, if Taylor didn't want to talk to me, if he didn't want to listen and try to understand, then fine. And CJ certainly didn't need to know about that—although he probably did, already.

But in the meantime, I still had to get the ball rolling. I was going to New York, to prove something to myself, to Taylor, and to Quinn, once and for all. And, however the pieces fell, I would deal with the consequences.

I made arrangements with Marva to take care of Jamel while I was gone, especially since I had no idea what Taylor's plans were. I didn't want to think about it. I left work early, picked up Jamel from day care and took him to Marva's house. The possibility of Taylor walking out on us was a concept I didn't want to imagine. Besides, if I gave into Taylor's real wish for me not to go to New York, what would be next? What else would he *not* want me to do, and hold the threat of leaving me over my head if I went against him?

That idea took root, giving me the last ounce of determination I needed to do what must be done. *Yeah, he had a lot of nerve.*

But even as I put my key in the door of the house that Ty and I shared, all the bravado in the world couldn't have prepared me for what I found.

TAYLOR

THREE

The Bed You Make

The past two days were hell—it's the only word to describe it, although I could probably think of something more graphic. The folks that worked for me were busy doing their computer thing all around me, but I wasn't really seeing them.

I was just sitting there trying to figure out where things had gone wrong between me and Max.

I should have known this day was coming, sooner or later. I figured I'd be prepared, that's all. But there was that part of me—maybe male ego, maybe plain stupidity—that made me think that Maxine and I had this perfect, incredible thing happening between us that would last forever. You know, like in the great American romances. Ha, what a joke. I guess she had other thoughts all along. That's the thing that's tearing me up inside. She was playing me.

Suddenly I felt as if I didn't know her anymore, what

she was about. That everything we'd been planning, handling, and dealing with on the day–to–day these past three years was all a crazy dream. It wasn't real, not if it could crumble to pieces with one phone call—make her start lying and hiding things from me.

Naw, it isn't right. I thought, *this whole thing is wrong, and it seems there isn't a damned thing I can do about it. So here I am, thirty–five–years–old, with my own business, a solid future, and it doesn't mean a thing.*

I looked up, and CJ was grinning down at me. "Hey, Man, you just going to stare at the computer screen all day, or what?" he asked me, punctuating his question with a slap on my back.

Calvin Jackson and I have been hard and fast running partners since sophomore year in high school. Man, the things we haven't done together could fit on the head of a pin. He's the closest thing to family I have.

"Just thinking, Man. That's all."

CJ pulled up a chair next to my desk and sat down. His brows knitted in concern.

"You look like a bad pot of grits, Man, all lumps and mush. I can give you a razor to get rid of that shadow, unless you're going for a new look."

I had to laugh. CJ came up with the most ridiculous visuals. "That bad, huh?"

"Yeah. That's the watered down version. What's happening? You been walking around like a zombie for days. You're not sick, are you?"

"Naw."

"Everything cool at home? 'Cause I know that business is booming. So that ain't it."

I looked away for a moment and stared at the web page design I'd been pretending to be working on for the past few hours.

CJ and I started WebMasters about five years ago, just the two of us. Now we have a staff of ten graphic designers and five technicians, and more business than we can handle. He was right. It wasn't business.

"It's Max," I blurted out, as if those two words would somehow explain everything.

"Is she all right, Man? *She's* not sick, or anything?"

I shook my head, almost wishing it were something that simple—that she could just take something—a pill, some cough syrup—and everything would be cool.

"No. She's not sick."

"Oh, that's good." He waited a beat. "So—what is it?"

I shut off my computer. Couldn't concentrate, anyway. "It's that brother from New York, Man."

CJ's eyes widened, then narrowed, in that look he always has seconds before he gets really pissed off.

"What about him? Don't tell me he's trying to make a move on Maxine. Not after all this time. That's bulls—"

"It's not him. At least not like that. It's Maxine, too."

"What!" He sat straight up in his seat. "Naw, you're gonna spell this one out for me, my brother. Not Max," he hissed between his teeth, then caught himself and took a sidelong glance around the office.

CJ had been the one who'd cautioned me from day one about getting involved with Maxine—especially with her being pregnant with another man's baby.

"Are you out of your mind, Ty?" he'd asked me one Sunday afternoon in the park after we both nearly collapsed from exhaustion after a game of one–on–one. "You don't know what you're getting yourself involved in. What if this Quinn dude pops back up and wants to lay claim? This is all rebound, man. You deserve better than that. Just chill a minute before you rush into this thing. I don't want to see you get all messed up."

I hadn't listened. I didn't want to.

From the first moment I laid eyes on Maxine, I knew she was my soulmate, the one person, who—after years of emotional denial and detachment—turned the light back on in my world. Maxine made me want to trust in being in love and loving again, something I'd thought could never happen. She'd opened her heart to me without expecting anything in return. At the same time, she needed me—and it had been far too long since I felt needed by anyone.

It all happened so suddenly, like an accident, nothing planned—not a blind date thing. It was as if fate had stepped in and said, "Here, Man, 'this Bud's for you.' "

How it went down was that we had just landed our first big client—a corporation with outlets in ten major cities across the country. They wanted us to design their website, as well as install computer systems at all of their locations. This was it. CJ and I had just hit the big time.

The CEO of the company wanted the two of us to fly down to Atlanta to meet with the execs from all of his locations, sign the deal, and start work as of yesterday.

CJ was busy pulling together our bag of tricks for our presentation, and I was assigned the task of handling the flight arrangements. Our hotel, ground transportation, and food were being taken care of on the other end, which was really cool.

There was a travel agency I passed every now and then on my way in and out of town. I believed it was black–owned, and I was all for keeping business "in the family," so I figured I'd give it a shot.

For the life of me, I couldn't remember the name of the place, so I went in person which was okay, too, since it was sort of on my way home.

I pulled up in front of the place about six–fifteen or so, just as a woman—who I later discovered was Marva—was hanging the CLOSED sign in the window.

Dashing across the street I ran up to the door and knocked on the glass.

The same woman who'd just hung up the sign came to

the door and mouthed, "We're closed." She had the most incredible blue eyes, set against pale skin.

Just as I put on my best "begging" expression and clasped my hands in prayer, the absolutely finest woman I'd seen in a while walked up behind her.

Being what I considered a connoisseur of gorgeous women, I knew this one was way up on the Richter scale.

She was a brown, svelte beauty, the color of mouthwatering chocolate, with a close-cut hairdo that framed her near-perfect face. She had wide, expressive brown eyes and full, kissable lips. Her body was a Playboy photographer's dream, with long dancer's legs displayed beneath a short denim skirt that had me thinking all kinds of wild thoughts. She wasn't busty but full, bringing to mind peaches, ripe and sweet for the picking.

She said something to the woman next to her, who stepped aside as the beauty opened the door.

"Hi. Can I help you?"

Her voice, rich and sweet as honey, slid all over me, and her smile with that little gap in front—oh, Man. I forced myself to concentrate on why I was there.

"I hope so. I know you're closed, but I'm desperate."

"We can't have that." She grinned. "Come in and let's see what we can work out. I'm Maxine Sherman," she said, leading the way into the small, but cozy office.

"Taylor Collins."

"I'm going to head home, Maxine. Will you be okay?" Blue eyes gave me a sideways glance.

"Sure, Marva. Go on. I'll see you in the morning."

"Goodnight," she said to both of us.

"Night," we harmonized, and turned to each other and laughed.

"So, where are you so desperate to go, Mr. Collins?" Maxine asked, taking a seat behind a cluttered desk.

"Atlanta. Day after tomorrow."

"That shouldn't be a problem. It'll just cost you a bit more. The short notice," she added by way of explanation.

"No problem, as long as I get there."

"Please, have a seat," she said, indicating a chair next to her desk, and I noticed the slenderness of her long fingers—and no rings.

She shuffled some papers around, actually moving them from one pile into another, and turned on her computer. With a few quick strokes of those lovely fingers she had the reservation screen up. She bit down on her lip in concentration as the information scrolled in front of her.

"There's a seven A.M. flight available through American Airlines. Is that okay?"

I forced myself to concentrate on what she was saying to keep from focusing on the smoothness of her skin, the sensual movement of her bare fingers, and the way her mouth became an erotic orifice every time she spoke.

"*Uh,* sure. That sounds find. I'll need two tickets. For my partner and I, Calvin," I added, for some reason, needing her to know that a woman wasn't involved.

She smiled. "When will you be returning?"

"At least a week. It's a business trip."

"Really? I can get you a good rate." She keyed in some more information. "What kind of business are you in?"

"Web design and computer installation and maintenance."

"That must keep you busy."

"Very." I smiled. "As a matter of fact, this trip is to close a deal with one of the first big clients we've had."

"Congratulations. I hope everything works out for you."

She continued to type in the information. "Can I arrange for hotel, or car rental?"

"No. The people we're going to see are taking care of that."

She smiled again, and I thought my heart had stood still.

"Aren't you lucky?"

"We've worked hard. It's been a struggle but things are finally coming together."

She leaned back a bit and looked at me. "I know the feeling." Her eyes roamed the space. "There were days when I first opened the agency that I thought I'd made a major mistake. But it was my dream, and I was determined to make it work."

I nodded, experiencing the same thought myself on too many occasions. If not for CJ convincing me to hang in there, I might have given up. Who did she have to cheer her on?

"You're not *from* here," I said after a moment, the rapid pronunciation of her words finally settling in.

"New York. I've been here about four years."

"No kidding? I visited there a couple of times. Tough city."

"That it is," she said in what sounded like a faraway voice.

"Miss it?"

"At times."

She looked away then, but not before I caught the flicker of some painful shadow in her eyes. Her open demeanor seemed to shut down, her body tense every so slightly. I was pretty good at reading body language. That said more to me than anything that came out of folks' mouths, which was generally whatever they wanted you to believe. But the body—now, that didn't lie—and Maxine's body was speaking all the words her lips refused to say. There was a history in New York, one which she'd chosen to put behind her, or so she thought.

She cleared her throat. "How will you be paying for your ticket—cash or charge?" she asked, now all business, the easy banter of moments ago gone in a key stroke.

"Charge. Visa." I reached into my back pocket, a bad

habit, and pulled out my wallet. I handed her my credit card.

"What's the last name of the other party, your partner?"

"Jackson. Calvin Jackson."

She processed the card without another word and handed it back. Moments later my tickets were printed out.

"Here you are."

She smiled, but the sparkle was gone from her eyes. I wanted to ask her what was wrong. *Was it something I'd said?* But some instinct told me to leave it alone.

And then all of a sudden she looked at me, her eyes glistening as if she were about to cry.

"You ever wish you could go back and do something over?" she asked, suddenly. "Something you'd really screwed up, something that maybe if you'd said something, had done something, everything would have been different?"

I wasn't sure where the question had come from, or where the conversation was heading, but I could see that this was no out of the blue inquiry that could be tossed off with some pat response. She really wanted—needed— an answer. A truthful one.

I thought about it for a moment. Yeah, there were definitely some episodes in my life that I'd like to go back and fix. Like the fact that I didn't know who my family was, or that the one woman who I'd finally given my heart to, Karen Long, had gotten rid of our baby that she'd carried.

"How can I have a baby from a man who doesn't even know who he is? Suppose there are some maniac genes or something in your family?" she'd said, as if she'd done nothing more than take out the garbage. Humph, garbage.

But maybe she was right. I *didn't* know, and had no way to prove otherwise. For as long as I lived I'd never be more than one big question mark.

That was almost six years ago, but the revelation took

its toll. From that day on, I never looked at relationships with women, family, or myself the same way. And I believed there was a part of me that would never be whole. How could I offer myself to anyone, when I didn't know who I really was?

"Yes," I finally answered, "but you can't go back. All you can do is deal with the reality, make the best of it, and move on."

She looked at me, wide-eyed and hopeful, and a place inside of me seemed to shift, crack open. I almost heard the hinges creak from lack of use. A part of me that had been dead—stirred, struggling for resurrection. But everything I was, had been, had ever been dealt, beat it back down.

Shoving the tickets into my shirt pocket, I stood. "Thank you for all your help. Sorry to have kept you. I'm sure there must be a family to go home to."

She hesitated a moment. "No. Just me."

Her answer pulled me up short. I couldn't imagine a woman like Maxine not having something waiting for her to walk through the door.

I slung my hands into my pants pockets, and for the life of me, right up to today, I don't know where the next words that fell out of my mouth came from.

"Hey, since, I kept you—if you don't have any plans—maybe we can go for a quick bite to eat."

She smiled, not a come-on smile or anything, but sort of shy and unsure.

"That's really nice of you, but I don't think so. Thank you, anyway."

I shrugged. "Hey, no problem. Just a thought. Thanks for your help." I turned to leave.

"Maybe some other time." It was more of a question than a statement, halting me mid-stride, cast out like bait on a hook.

I turned back around, and there was that half–smile again.

I nodded. "Cool. Some other time, then. Maybe when I get back from Atlanta."

"Okay."

"Take care, Maxine."

"You, too."

The entire week that CJ and I spent in Atlanta, all I could think about was Maxine. I couldn't quite put my finger on whatever it was about her that had hit me. Maybe it was that moment of vulnerability I saw in her eyes, or the sensation that she'd stirred in me that made me want to take care of her and protect her—even though she seemed to have it all together, cloaked in an undeniable aura of sensuality.

Whatever it was, I couldn't seem to shake it, and the realization unnerved me. For too long I didn't allow myself to experience any real feelings for a woman, and I wasn't sure what to do with them now, how to handle it. I figured I'd rap with CJ about it. Even though he wasn't married or anything, he'd been hooked up with Tracy for what seemed like forever. What was always cool about my friendship with CJ over the years was that we could always be honest with each other, even about the dumbest stuff, how we felt from deep inside, crazy ideas we had, the things that scared us. And it was always cool.

CJ was the only person besides me who knew the real deal about me and my family, how it made me feel like half a man not knowing who they were, and what Karen had done to our baby. No one but CJ knew how that almost destroyed me, but he hung in there with me, stayed solid, stayed my man.

But even for me, trying to explain what was going on with this chick Maxine was a bit much.

We were sitting in the hotel bar in Atlanta, relaxing, taking in the sights and sounds. CJ was on his second screwdriver, while I nursed my rum and coke. Can't quite say when we decided these were our drinks of choice. Maybe one of those Saturday night basement parties from back in the day—the ones where it was black as pitch, with the purple light that made all the lint show up on our clothes, and almost all of the music was slow so that we could grind with our girls up against the wall or in some corner, and B.Y.O.B.B. was a requirement for entry. Yeah, maybe it was one of those. But that's another story.

Anyway, CJ and I were just kicking it, not talking about anything special, just some of the stuff we needed to be ready for the next day, when CJ spotted these two fine sisters sliding onto the stools on the opposite side from us.

"Hmm. Check them out," he said over the rim of his glass.

I looked. One reminded me of Iman, the super model, and the other looked like an older version of Brandy, the singer. Neither one of them looked like Maxine. Maybe Iman, around the eyes.

"Not bad," I said.

"Not bad! Brother, are you blind?"

"Not the last time I checked. Just not interested. And with Tracy back in Frisco waiting for you, you shouldn't be interested, either."

He gave me a hard, get ready to rumble look, but knowing that those days were behind him I just ignored it.

"You know, Ty, I hate it when you're right." He took a sip of his drink. "But hey, just because I'm in love doesn't mean I have to roll over and play dead." He chuckled and ordered another drink. "My eyes are still workin,' even if my heart is under lock and key." He patted his chest for extra drama.

I glanced at him for a moment, and knew from the faraway look in his eyes that he was thinking about Tracy. That was my opening.

"CJ, Man—"

"Yeah?"

"How did you know that Tracy was the one for you?"

The corner of his mouth curved up in a slow grin. "Hmm." He took another sip of his refreshed drink. "Sometimes I think it was when we first made love." He shut his eyes for a minute and shook his head. "Blew my mind. But then other times I think that couldn't have been it, because it wouldn't have been that fantastic if everything else wasn't already in place." He turned to me. "Know what I mean?"

"Yeah."

"Humph. Other times I think it was our first kiss, or the time we both cut out from work and had a picnic in the park."

His brows rose and fell in thought. "But I guess it was the way she made me feel almost from the moment I met her, Man. It was just easy and right, like we'd been waiting all our lives for that day. Something just clicked."

He angled his head in my direction and flashed me that scowl again.

"Why, Bro? Think you've run into Ms. Heavensent?"

I shrugged. "Maybe."

"Oh, no." He chuckled. "You're not gettin' off that light. Let's hear it. Who is she, and why haven't I met her?"

"I just met her myself—at the travel agency when I went to get our tickets."

"And—"

"And that's it." I took a long swallow of my drink.

"Oh no it isn't. I know you just want to spill your guts. So you might as well get it over with."

I could feel his gaze burning into the side of my face. He wasn't going to let up until I told him, and I wanted to, anyway.

"I don't know, Man," I said, trying to find a way to

explain what was going on in my head. Then it dawned on me. "I guess it's like what happened with you and Tracy. Something just clicked."

CJ just stared at me, seemingly at a loss for a quick comeback, which was his usual style.

"Man, don't sit there looking at me like I have two heads."

He started cracking up. "Ty, Man, I never thought I'd see the day when something *clicked* for you. I always figured you'd stay on the prowl until they had to cart you away. Tracy is going to love this. Now maybe she can stop playing matchmaker."

Tracy's mission in life was to hook me up with everyone from her second cousin and her hairdresser to her sorority sisters. If nothing else, she was persistent. Should things work out with me and Maxine, then maybe I could safely visit CJ on a Saturday night without the fear of a setup in the works.

CJ tossed down the last of his drink, and then grew serious. He turned to me. "So, what's she like—"

We returned to Frisco late in the day Friday and, like a man possessed, the first thing I did when I dropped my bags at the foot of my bed was to call the travel agency.

"Sherman Travel. May I help you?"

I started to hang up. It was probably a stupid idea, calling like that. She was probably just being nice when she said—

"Hello? May I help you? Hello?"

"Uh, hello. I was trying to reach ... Maxine ... Sherman."

"Hold on, please."

Oh, man, this was not a good idea. I felt like a total idiot.

"Hello?"

That voice again. My insides started to knot up. "Hello, Maxine?"

"Yes. Who's this?"

"Taylor Collins, from the other day. I bought the tickets—"

"Hi! How are you?"

She actually sounded happy to hear from me. The knot started to loosen. "Fine. Just got back in."

"How was your trip?"

"Hectic, but productive. Thanks for working things out for me."

"Please . . . no problem. It's what we do."

"So, how have you been?" I asked, feeling more ridiculous by the minute.

"Incredibly busy."

I heard her soft laughter and it made me smile. "That must mean business is good."

"Absolutely. I'm not complaining."

We were both quiet for a moment. I could hear voices in the background and I guessed her assistant, Marva, was tapping on the computer keys for a customer.

"I, *uh,* guess I should let you get back to work. I know you're busy."

"Okay. It was good hearing from you. I'm glad you had a successful trip."

"Thanks again."

"Sure."

We both seemed to be suspended in air, holding our breath, hoping that the drop wouldn't be fatal. Then we both spoke at once.

"Taylor, I—"

"I was hoping I could—" We both laughed. "Ladies first."

She cleared her throat, then hesitated as if maybe she'd changed her mind. "I thought maybe if you weren't busy tomorrow night, there's an outdoor jazz concert in the park—"

I chuckled. "I was getting ready to ask you the same thing."

"So I guess that's a yes?" I could almost hear the smile in her voice.

"Definitely. Maybe we could grab a bite before show-time, then head on over."

"I have a better idea. I, *uh*, try to be careful what I eat . . . these days. So why don't I fix some snacks and we can take them to the park?"

"Well, I don't want to just be bringing my long arms. What can I do?"

"Hmmm. Bring a blanket and something to drink. Juice or water," she added quickly.

Guess she didn't drink, I thought, and stored the infor-mation away. "No problem. I think I can handle that. Is six good?"

"Fine."

I let out a relieved breath. "So . . . I'll see you tomorrow at six."

"Yes. Six. I'm working tomorrow, so you can pick me up here."

"Yeah, me too. I'll be there. Goodnight, Maxine."

"Night."

And it was then I knew I wanted to say goodnight to Maxine every night of my life.

By the time I pulled up across the street from Sherman Travel for my date with Maxine, I was shaking like some-thing with a bad case of the willies. I'd been pretty much useless at work, couldn't stay focused. All I could think about was that I wanted tonight to be perfect. I knew I was acting like this was the first time I'd been out with a woman, which was far from true, but I couldn't get rid of that twitchy sensation in my stomach. And if CJ said, "Just be cool," one more time, we would have come to blows.

"Maybe Tracy and I'll come and check you out at the park," he'd said just before we got ready to head out for the day.

Although most computer firms did the regular five day, nine to five, WebMasters was a twenty–four hour, seven day a week operation. I couldn't count the times in the beginning when we got calls at home in the middle of the night from clients whose systems went down. After a few months of that, we decided to expand the hours. Then it was days. It was rough at first with the small staff, but now twenty–four–seven was a way of life.

"Do I look like I need a chaperone, CJ? I know good and well you and Tracy have something else to do beside peep over my shoulder."

"We dig jazz too, Man. You tryin' to tell me we can't come?" he asked, attempting to sound hurt. "It's a free country, ya know? I can go wherever—"

"CJ—shut up."

He cracked up laughing. "Man," he blew out over his laughter, "whatever Ms. Thing whispered in your ear, my brother, has you all twisted. I'm scared to see what's gonna happen to you if you get this thing going. Look at you. You haven't been right all day. Matter of fact, what day is it?"

"I'm glad you think this is funny. Anything to amuse my audience."

"Naw, Man. I'm sorry. Really." He chuckled again. "It's just that this is so unlike you. You've been the ice man for the past three, four years. But Ms. Travel Agent has certainly pressed the defrost button."

I thought about that as I drove to pick up Maxine. CJ was right. Maxine had pressed some kind of button. I had to pull myself together, though. Damn, I wasn't asking her to marry me, or something. We were just going to a concert in the park. *Can't get any more benign than that,* I thought, finding a quick parking space.

Jogging across the street, I just missed getting my unfocused self hit by a Dodge Caravan. I pulled myself together right quick as I walked up to the door. I could see her through the plate glass window that took up the whole left side of the building.

She was on the phone. Smiling. And typing something into her computer. She was prettier than I remembered. There was a glow about her that couldn't be duplicated with makeup, a softness about her that made my insides shift. *Okay, buddy, this is it,* I thought. I stepped up to the door and rang the bell.

Maxine looked toward the door and smiled. I heard the sound of a buzzer, and the door clicked. I went inside.

"Hi. Be right with you," she mouthed, still talking on the phone. She pointed to the chair by her desk, motioning me to sit, which I did.

I looked around, really looked this time, taking inventory of my surroundings. As travel agencies went, this one was pretty nice. Of course it was filled with paraphernalia of all the exotic places in the world one could visit. But there were personal touches, too that I hadn't noticed before—like the plants that hung from the ceiling, the art work of Tom Feelings that hung on the walls, or the rack of coffee mugs, none of which matched, that sat on a table in the corner. Music was coming from somewhere, but I didn't see any speakers. "Mr. Magic," by Grover Washington was on. I started tapping my foot to the beat, trying to relax.

"Whew. Sorry I took so long," she said, hanging up the phone.

She gave me that smile again, and there was the little toothpick–wide gap between her front teeth. It was kind of cute.

"Almost. Are you ready?"

"Just about. I need to print these tickets out for another

last minute client." She gave me a playful look. "I have to Fed Ex them so they can reach the client by tomorrow. It should only take a few more minutes. Do you mind?"

"Of course not. Take care of business." I grinned. "Or you won't have one."

"You're right about that. Glad you understand."

I looked at her for a moment, curious. "Why wouldn't I?"

She glanced up from what she was doing and shrugged slightly. "I don't know. Some men have a problem with women running their own businesses, especially if it takes time away from them."

She peered at me from beneath her lashes.

"Is that your experience?" I asked.

"Not me, personally. But I know women who've run up against it."

"Hmm." I leaned back a bit. "I hope I didn't give you that impression. I think it's great when a woman does her own thing—a sense of independence and vision."

"Really?"

She looked at me as if my answer held the key to some age old secret.

"Yes. Really."

I saw her release a breath, then slowly nod her head, a soft smile on her lips. "A renaissance man."

"Oh, hello."

We both turned at the sound of the voice. It was blue eyes.

"Hey, Marva. Marva, this is Taylor Collins. Taylor, my assistant and best friend, Marva Torino."

I stood as she approached, coming, I concluded, from some unseen room beyond the main office.

"Nice to meet you, Taylor. Formally."

"You, too."

Her hand was as soft as velvet, and she had a great smile to go with those eyes.

"So, I hear you two are going to the concert tonight."

"Yes." I looked at Maxine, and could have sworn she'd just blushed.

"I love McCoy Tyner. But Brent didn't feel like doing anything tonight."

"You're welcome to come with us," I offered, trying to be nice, but praying she'd say no.

"And sit up under you two. No thanks." She laughed.

I was relieved. "If you're sure."

"Definitely. Besides, I know Brent and I will find something to do to entertain ourselves."

She gave me a wink and a smile.

"Marva!" Maxine giggled.

"What? What did I say?" she asked with an innocent note in her voice. "Just because we've been married for seven years doesn't mean we don't have the itch. Got to keep the home fires burning. Know what I mean?"

"Absolutely," I agreed, liking her open style.

"See?" She pinned Maxine with a triumphant look. "Anyway, the receipts are all taken care of. I'll make the deposit on my way home."

"Thanks, Girl. Would you mind taking these tickets to the Federal Express office? It's totally out of our way, and I don't want to sit around waiting for them to come for a pickup."

"Sure. What time is the show, anyway?"

"Eight." Maxine handed Marva the envelope.

"You two have a great time tonight."

"Thanks." I stood. "Good meeting you."

"Hope to see you again, Taylor."

She looked from me to Maxine.

"So do I."

"Night, Maxie. Have a good weekend. See you Monday," she added, and headed for the door. "Bye, Taylor."

She was on the other side of the door before I could respond. I turned to Maxine. "Interesting woman."

She laughed. "That's an understatement."

"You two been friends long?" I was curious about Maxine's friendship, which was apparently close, being with a white woman. Not that it was impossible, but Maxine gave me the impression that she was, at the heart of it, a girl from the neighborhood. There was a real urban air about her. Marva came off cool, but slightly pampered. The pairing of the two was interesting. Although I'd met many white folks and even had several on staff, I'd never found myself in a close personal relationship with one.

"Wow, let's see," Maxine said, cutting into my thoughts. "Marva walked in the door about three months after I opened the office, *told* me I needed her help and she was ready to start right then. And she did."

She started to laugh. "That girl is a whirlwind. She really helped me get the business into shape. Prior to getting her travel agency license she'd done some marketing work for a firm in San Diego. Before that she kept the accounting books for a boutique. She put all of her energy into spreading the word about Sherman Travel. A lot of door–to–door and phone calls. It really helped a lot. Before I knew it, we had more business than we could handle, and that's where her accounting skills come into play. She's great with numbers, and she's good with people." She paused a moment. "And she's been there for me when I really needed her."

Her gaze drifted off for a moment. She blinked, then turned to me. "Everybody should have a friend like her. She reminds me of my homegirl Val, from New York—diehard loyal." She turned off her computer.

"Sounds like my buddy, CJ."

"The one you went to Atlanta with?"

"Yeah."

"Friends are important. Especially when you don't have family."

She piled some papers in a stack on her desk, really only

moving them from one side to the other. I'd noticed that the last time I was there. I guess it made her feel as if she'd actually straightened up her desk. It made me smile. *A quirky habit.*

"I'll get our goodies from the fridge and we can go."

I didn't see one in the immediate vicinity, so I assumed it was in the mysterious back room.

I watched her walk away, my thoughts still attached to her earlier statement about family. Did she mean that about herself, or was she just talking in generalities? If anyone did, I knew what it was like to be without family. Maybe we'd get a chance to talk about it later.

"All set."

I jumped up and took the red–and–white cooler that she was pulling into the room, which appeared to be almost as big as she was.

"What do you have in here?" I asked, surprised by the weight of the thing.

"Everything you could think of for an outdoor concert under the stars," she said with a dramatic flair.

I laughed. "In that case, let's get moving. I'm more anxious to see what you have stashed away in there than I am to hear the concert." I waited at the door while she programmed the alarm.

"I can guarantee you'll enjoy it."

And I did.

The night was perfect, nearly cloudless with the temperature in the low eighties, a light breeze blowing just right. Stars twinkled in between the leaves of the overhanging trees, playing hide–and–seek while appearing close enough to touch.

The park was a quilt of color from one end to the next. Blankets in every design dotted the grass–covered slopes, as well as long and short–limbed bodies in everything from teasing, tight spandex to khaki and denim.

The smell of smoke drifted then hung suspended over

heads—the kind of smoke you couldn't buy at your local grocery store, and the kind you could.

For as far as the eye could see, there was representation of nationalities from Asian to Caucasian, and everything in between. Even though everyone was out to hear a concert, it was as if they wanted to be sure they heard music—any music. Everything from hip–hop to the classics could be heard in a montage of convoluted sound that melded together almost as if it should.

Humph—music, the great equalizer.

Maxine and I found a great spot, dead center, with a perfect view of the stage and the exits. And she was right about the contents of the cooler. There was a feast inside. Man, a woman who knew the way to my heart. I was in love.

"Here's my meager contribution." I opened my duffel bag and took out the jug of juice, two bottles of water and a thermos of ice.

She smiled. "Perfect."

The consummate hostess, Maxine laid the containers out on the blanket, assembling everything within easy reach, then settled back.

"Help yourself."

I wanted to kiss her. I didn't. Instead, I did as I was instructed. It was safer, anyway.

Just as we began to dig in, the MC came on stage and the show began.

For the next two hours I allowed myself to fall under Maxine's spell: her soft laughter, the alluring scent of her, the sparkle in her eyes, her witty observations about the people around us. And it wasn't that she was trying to win me over. Everything about her seemed natural, real.

About halfway through, I'd settled myself against a tree and eased Maxine against me, her back pressed against my chest. At first I felt her reluctance from the tightness of her body, the way she held herself ever so slightly away from me. But slowly I felt her relax and let go, until resting against me seemed like the most natural thing in the world. I pressed my chin against the top of her head and closed my eyes a minute, swaying just a little to the music. Yeah, this was nice.

Since we'd decided to take my car to the concert, I drove Maxine back to her office to pick up her ride. We stood in front of her Honda Accord.

"I had a great time tonight, Taylor. Thank you."

She briefly lowered her gaze, almost as if she were surprised, or felt she was undeserving of being entertained.

"So did I. You're wonderful company, and you make a mean potato salad."

She laughed, and I stuck my hands into the pockets of my jeans to keep from touching her. She looked up at me.

"I—should be getting home."

"Yeah. I guess you have plans for tomorrow, huh?"

"Nothing special. Sunday is usually my lazy day. I'll probably go to church in the morning, and that's about it."

"Well, if you feel like it, give me a call. Maybe we can see a movie, or something."

She hesitated, as if she had to weigh the right and wrong of it. She bit down on her lip, like I'd seen her do before when she was thinking.

"I don't have your number," she finally said. "It's on my Rolodex in the office."

I almost shouted Amen. "Got a pen?"

She dug in her purse and handed me a pen and a piece of paper.

"Call whenever."

She glanced at the number. "I will. Goodnight, Taylor." She turned to open her car door.

"Maxine."

"Yes?"

She turned halfway, and I stepped up to her. Her eyes

widened just a bit, and I was up close enough to feel the warmth from her body.

"I want to kiss you."

"Taylor . . . I—"

"Just say yes, Maxine."

She seemed so afraid, scared to explore. I wanted her to trust me. I wanted to take that frightened, haunted look out of her eyes.

Her gaze danced across my face. Her lips parted slightly, and then she slowly nodded.

And that first kiss was everything I thought it would be. Heavensent.

After that first night, it was as if my world opened again. I wanted to take a chance on being with someone. I wanted to do more than just work until I was exhausted, or spend my free time bar hopping, or being set up with one of Tracy's inexhaustible supply of friends. I wanted to be with Maxine.

I looked forward to the end of my day so that we could be together. Usually during the week we met after work, had dinner and maybe saw a movie, stopped by a comedy club, or listened to some jazz. Sometimes we'd take a tour of the plethora of antique shops, and I swear Maxine knew where they all were. She was a chronic antique shopper who found the greatest deals.

"Some day I'm going to stumble across a real treasure in one of these musty, dusty places," she'd said. "And I'm going to be rich. And then, maybe, you'll appreciate the fine art of scavenging." She laughed and kissed me on the lips—light as a feather. She did that a lot, and I loved it.

I slid my arms around her waist. "You're going to have to teach me some of your scavenging tricks," I said. "How will I know if I've really found something worthwhile? How do you know?"

She gazed up at me, her lips slightly parted, and that tiny gap in her teeth peeked at me. She reached out and ran her index finger along the line of my jaw.

"You know a treasure when you find it," she said. "Something inside of you gets a warm, tingling feeling, like the thrill of climbing to the peak of the roller coaster and looking down—the same sensation I felt when I found you." She smiled, trailed her finger across my lips, then said, "Come on, there are three more shops I want to check out."

All I could do was shake my head and savor the pleasure ride of Maxine. It was things like that, words she said, a look, a touch, that made the difference, strengthening the bond.

The more time I spent with her the better she made me feel. Yet, as good as it was, there was a part of herself that she held back. For all her humor, the drive, intelligence, and what I felt was a genuine, giving nature, there was that sumthin' sumthin' in Maxine that I couldn't reach. And not knowing why rattled me. . . .

FOUR

No Turning Back

"Ready to cut out, Man?" CJ asked one day, successfully interrupting my thoughts of Maxine.

He'd eased alongside my desk and sat on the edge, his dark shades perched perilously on the bridge of his broad nose. He thought it was cool.

"Yeah. In a minute. Just need to put these figures in," I said. "What's happening on the Atlanta project?"

We were fifty–fifty partners. CJ handled all installations and maintenance along with the crew, and my role was design and administration, which worked out fine for both of us.

He put a manila folder on my desk. *The report.*

"Just got it from Reggie."

I opened the folder, and as always, Reggie's assessment was meticulous. Reggie was our senior technician—twenty years old, and just plain ole brilliant. I'd met him about two years earlier when he'd *"Pssst, psssted"* at me from a corner, trying to sell me an electronic organizer.

"This here is special," he'd said, all long legs, arms, and a slick street grin.

"Yeah. What's special about it?"

"Found it in the street. Wasn't working, so I opened the sucker up and fixed it. Works like new. For you, twenty bucks. No tax." He chuckled.

I stared at him for a moment, not really sure why I didn't just walk away from this obvious hustler, or worse. The too big jeans, oversized shirt and Air Jordan kicks were all standard issue. He was definitely from the 'hood. I started to just blow him off. But there was something beneath the challenging stance, and the hardness of his young face. *Intelligence behind his eyes.* That's what I saw, and the underlying sense of pride in his voice when he told me he'd fixed the organizer.

He adjusted his long body, ready for whatever came his way—run, fight, didn't matter.

"What else can you do, kid?"

His dark, predatory eyes narrowed in momentary suspicion, trying to gauge me. Then he shrugged his right shoulder.

"Anything electronic. Computers mostly."

"You have a job?"

"Why?"

"I might have something for you to do."

"Legal?"

I laughed. "Yes. Very."

Humph. Now my man felt and looked good in a suit and tie, and could run a meeting as if he'd been nursed on Wall Street. There wasn't anyone in the company who could hold a candle to him when it came to knowing his stuff. I took a chance back then. *We* took a chance, and it paid off. Haven't regretted a day of having him on board.

I closed the folder and stuck it in my briefcase. "I'll take it home and look at it over the weekend."

"What's up for the weekend, anyway? You want to stop

by tomorrow, maybe play a little one–on–one? You're due for a butt kicking right about now."

I chuckled. I could waste CJ on the court with my eyes closed, and he knew it. "In your dreams, my brother. Anyway, I'm not too sure about tomorrow. I might try to get together with Maxine."

His left brow arched.

"How many weeks has this been, my man? Four? Five?"

"Six."

"So, when am I gonna really meet her? These brief chats on the phone when she calls here and glimpses of her from the passenger seat of your car don't constitute meeting your lady. Plus, Tracy has to give her the seal of approval. You know that, Brother."

I started laughing, even as the reality of what he was saying pushed what I'd been avoiding to the surface. Maybe an assessment from an outside party would tell me things I didn't want to know. If I could just keep Maxine to myself a little longer, maybe I could discover what the thin veil was that hung between us. I wasn't sure I was ready for anyone else to pull it down—not if I wasn't prepared for what was behind it.

"We could hook up the grill," he was saying. "We could have that game, and the ladies could chat—get to know each other."

I thought about it for a minute. "Sounds like a plan. I'll check with Maxine and let you know."

He nodded. Then his voice got quiet.

"You really dig her, don't you?"

I glanced up and knew, as always, it was okay. "Yeah. A lot."

He patted my shoulder. "So long as she makes you happy, Ty. That's what's important."

"She does."

"Then you're almost home, Brother." He grinned. "Just

need to decide if you want to round third, or hang out at second base."

Yeah. I knew just what he meant. It was all about taking chances. I packed up and we walked out together.

"So let me know about tomorrow," CJ said when we reached the parking lot.

"I'll call you in the A.M."

He stuck the key into the door of his battered Volvo. "Make it early."

"First thing." I opened the door of my Acura Legend— a present to myself when we launched the business, rides like a cloud—and slid onto the cream–colored leather seat.

"Later, Man."

"Later, CJ."

He pulled off in a puff of dust and I rolled out right behind him, heading in the opposite direction. I was still a little unsure about bringing Maxine to his house, but hey, no time like the present, as my grandma would've said had I known her.

I decided to go home first, take a quick shower and change instead of heading straight to Maxine's. I punched her number into my cell phone—didn't want her to think I wasn't coming—and put her on speaker.

"Hello?"

Loved that little hitch in her voice when she answered the phone. It made me smile. "Hi. It's Taylor."

"Hi. Is something wrong?"

"No. I want to run home first. Then I'll be over."

"Oh. No problem."

"Decide what you want to do tonight?" I heard her sigh.

"I was thinking maybe we could stay in tonight. I'm kind of tired, Ty."

I frowned. She didn't sound right. Not her usual sunny self. "Are you all right, Maxine?"

"Sure. Just a long day."

"Hey, listen, we could get together tomorrow, or Sunday. It's—"

"No. I want to see you." She paused. "Actually—I need to talk with you, Ty."

My stomach muscles tightened. "About what?"

"It'll keep until you get here."

"Don't I even get a hint?"

Her laughter sounded forced. "We'll talk when you get here."

I knew I wasn't going to get any more out of her, so I left it alone. "Want me to bring anything?"

"I thought I'd fix dinner for us. You could bring a movie."

If she was fixing dinner and wanted to catch a movie, I figured she wasn't going to toss me to the curb when I arrived.

"Anything special?"

"I haven't seen *Love Jones.*"

"*Love Jones* it is, then. As a matter of fact, why don't you let *me* fix dinner?"

"You?"

"Yes, me. You sound surprised."

She laughed. "I am."

"Brother has to eat. And take–out can get a little expensive."

"What can you cook?"

Skepticism was simmering in her voice, like stew in a pot set on low. I could almost visualize her squinting her brown eyes, trying to see through some scam.

"I can cook plenty of stuff. I'm a man of many talents."

She waited a beat. "Okay. Just nothing too heavy."

"I know. You want to keep that gorgeous figure." I chuckled, but what I really wanted to do was lick my lips just thinking about her. It was then that I realized there was dead silence on the other end. "Max?"

"Hmm?"

"Is everything all right? The tone in your voice hasn't been right since we got on the phone."

"Ty—" She blew out a breath that sounded like a cross between frustration and resignation. "I'd really rather wait and talk to you in person."

I was getting a really bad feeling, but I told myself: *Just chill. No sense in speculating.* "All right. I'll be there in about an hour."

"See you then."

As I hung up the phone the sound of her voice rested in the center of my chest, reminding me of the sudden calm the instant before reality hits and the wailing begins.

Twitchy. That's how I felt when I pulled up in front of her town house. I wasn't sure what was waiting for me on the other side of the door. What I did know was that it couldn't be good.

I sat there for a few minutes, getting myself together. But, bottom line, I'd never know what the deal was if I kept sitting there. Grabbing the two bags of groceries, I eased toward the lion's den.

When Maxine opened the door and I looked at her face and into her eyes, all I felt inside was that I didn't want to lose her. The sensation rushed through me so suddenly that my head felt momentarily light, but I couldn't let her know that.

"Hi, Taylor."

"Hi, yourself." I bent just a little and kissed her cheek. "What's in the bags?"

She tried to peek inside, but I snatched them away.

"No hints for me, no hints for you." I brushed by her and went inside, heading for the kitchen. I'd meant for the comment to be light and offense–free, but when I got to the threshold of the kitchen and turned Maxine was still standing there in the hallway, as if she'd been dismissed without cause.

The narrow hallway appeared to swallow her petite frame, closing in around her. She suddenly looked so fragile, ready to crumble into a million tiny pieces. That wasn't the Maxine Sherman I'd come to know.

I walked back toward her, feeling as if I were in a dream. You know, the kind when you're heading for your destination but no matter how hard you try the goal keeps moving farther away, even though it seems as if it's right there?

Slowly she raised her head, and our gazes collided. Her smile wobbled around the edges. Standing in front of her, I lifted her chin with the tip of my finger.

"Talk to me, Maxine. Please. Whatever it is, I can handle it. Just don't do this cloak and dagger stuff. It's killing me."

She sucked on the corner of her bottom lip, then took my hand. "Let me help you with dinner," she whispered. "We can talk in the kitchen."

Deciding not to push her for the time being, I followed her into the kitchen and we unpacked the bags I'd brought with me, laying the contents on the island counter. In silence.

Periodically I looked across the divide, snatching glances at her. Her expression was closed—unreadable—but her body movements were tight, rigid, as if she were afraid that if she didn't keep complete control she'd fall apart. What was it? What could be so important, the big secret? This wasn't like Maxine. She was always pretty up front with me. I'd seen her bloom, from cautious and hesitant to carefree and open. The biggest unknown was how what she had to tell me was going to affect us. Somehow I knew that whatever it was, it would.

I kept doing my thing, dicing some scallions and tomatoes while she seasoned the salmon steak—my specialty—with dried herbs from her garden, waiting for her to open up.

Music from the stereo in the living room drifted out to us, filling the gaps of silence while we worked.

Under other circumstances, all this rather innocent activity could have been comfortably pleasant. It was anything but. The tension vibrated in the air, crackling against the waves of music.

Just when I thought I'd snap like a dried branch, she started talking. Caught me totally off guard.

"When I was about six," she began, keeping her gaze focused on the food as if it were a crystal ball, "I was living in Harlem, in New York, and I met this girl, Lacy in my first grade class."

A soft smile moved slowly across her mouth like dawn breaking over the horizon.

"We became the best of friends. Well, the three of us did. She had a twin brother—Quinten. Mostly everyone called him Quinn. He let me and Lacy call him Q."

I was pretty sure I didn't like where this was heading, and I wanted her to hurry up and get to the bad news, get it over with. But I held my tongue and diced a little faster.

"Anyway, the three of us were really tight," she continued, "but when we were about sixteen, their mother disappeared. Actually, she walked out on them, and Q—Quinn—had to find ways to take care of himself and his sister. We were always scared the social workers or somebody were going to come and take them away. But Quinn got a guy, Remy, to be their guardian. In exchange, Quinn worked for him."

"Who was Remy?" I asked, not so much because I really wanted to know but because I needed to slow down this freight train of bad news that was barreling down on me. All of a sudden I didn't want to jump on board.

"He ran some clubs in the neighborhood. He paid Quinn pretty good for—running errands and stuff."

She looked up briefly, then back to what she was doing. She lined the glass baking pan with my dicings and a little margarine, placed the salmon steaks on top, and put the pan in the oven.

"Three–fifty should be good," I said, needing to say something to put a touch of reality back into this nightmare that was unfolding.

She adjusted the dial, then turned back to the counter and began wiping it down with a damp cloth, totally lost in thought.

"Is that it?"

She shook her head and let out a long breath.

"Anyway, over the years I guess I—developed a crush on him. I never said anything, though, but Lacy knew and so did our friend Valerie." She half smiled. "They always told me I should say something and let him know how I felt. But Quinn treated me like a sister—family. I didn't think he felt any real interest in me . . . not like . . . that. So I kept my mouth shut. And then Lacy was killed. Shot dead in the street coming home from church."

The muscles in her face trembled, and I saw her eyes get all shiny.

"I'm . . . sorry, Max. Really."

She just pressed her lips together and nodded her head.

"After that, everything changed. Quinn wasn't the same person anymore. Neither was I. But we started working together to find out the truth about Lacy's death. It . . . it seemed to bring us closer together, somehow, you know?"

She looked up at me, her eyes so sad, begging me to understand. I wasn't sure I did, or wanted to, not exactly. But I did know how tragedy could change a person. It had changed me. I nodded, hoping it would help.

She fidgeted with the cloth, folding it into a perfect square, then unfolded it and started over again.

"Then he met this girl. Nikita."

The slight edge of bitterness in her tone surprised me. It wasn't like her.

"And before anybody knew what happened they were an item, and our friendship slowly evaporated. Finally, I decided I needed to get away, get a new start, so I moved out here and opened the agency. Not too long after I got here and settled Quinn called, saying he was coming out here. At first I thought it was just for a visit. But he wound up staying, and it was like the friendship we once shared in New York was reborn."

She reached down into the cabinet beneath the counter and took out a medium-size pot, filled it with some water and a little olive oil, and put it on the stove on a low flame.

So basically I figured she was trying to tell me they were still together—or something. But where was he? We'd been seeing each other for more than a month, and there were no signs of another man. Ever. Maybe they'd had a lover's quarrel and now he was back, wanting to patch things up. Maybe she'd been tipping around with him all along. No. Not Max. She wouldn't do that. But she had this look on her face, like there was more and she couldn't decide how to explain. I needed to know. Now.

"What are you telling me, Maxine? You want to get back together with this guy? You *are* with this guy? Is that the deal? Because if it is, just say so."

"No. That's not it."

She fidgeted with that damned cloth again.

"He's married."

For a minute the weight that had landed on my chest eased completely away. How do you spell relief? M-a-r-r-i-e-d. I held onto that one piece of good news—

"Ty . . . I . . . I'm pregnant."

Air rushed out of my lungs as if I'd been punched in the gut. Her words scrambled in my head, and my stomach started dancing. I know I didn't hear her right. *I* hadn't touched her. Not like that. So *it* wasn't possible. *We* hadn't been together. My mind was racing for answers, but nothing came into focus.

I looked at her and she was standing there with her arms wrapped around her waist, tears streaming down her cheeks. Maxine. *My Maxine*. Pregnant.

I finally snapped, feeling crazed, and asked the only thing that made any sense at the moment. "Whose is it?"

"Quinn's."

Everything suddenly stood still. "Quinn's? You said he was married—"

"He is."

"What are you telling me—you slept with a married man? What?"

Her body jerked from the assault of my voice. She gripped the edge of the counter, lowered her head a moment, then looked straight at me.

"I . . . I didn't find out I was pregnant until after he was gone—a week before he got married."

She started breathing hard. Her nostrils flared as if she were struggling for air. I saw her fighting back another rush of tears, but I wasn't sure what to do—go to her and tell her everything would be all right, tell her as if I were her man? Or was I just a friend? I didn't know anymore.

Putting down the knife, I looked across the counter at her. She was beautiful, funny, tender, intelligent. Everything a man could want in a woman. Everything I could want. Maxine put the sun back in my life. I'd fallen in love with her, and it was as if I'd been awakened from a deep sleep.

I understand that now as I stood there staring at her, wanting her, needing her in my life, and at the same time realizing that she was carrying another man's child. *Another man's child*. All at once the light began to dim, and I felt myself slipping back to that dark place, the place where my heart was cold, my feelings distant—somewhere I'd never thought I'd be again. Until that moment.

Tightness gripped my throat, spread to my chest, and made my stomach rock. I wanted to scream, hit something, someone—anything to make this thing that was going on inside of me go away.

I'd been tossed out to sea with no life preserver. And if I didn't find a way to stop myself from drifting away, I knew there'd be no getting back.

Turning, I walked away, feeling like a man of a hundred years. Everything ached from the inside out. I kept going until I found myself in the downstairs bathroom.

Shutting the door, I released the shudders that I'd fought to contain. I couldn't remember the last time I'd felt like crying, screaming, hurting someone. I guess it was when Karen walked out after telling me she'd killed our baby. I closed my eyes. Suddenly, Karen's face mocked me, laughed at the fool I'd been made of, once again. "I'm not a fool!"

I slammed my fist against the wall, and the pain stunned me as it shot up my arm and radiated through my body. I thought all feelings had left me, died with Maxine's admission. I'd trusted Maxine. I'd put my emotions into her hands and she'd used me, just like Karen, wound me up until she had my feelings on a string, under her control. I'd been nothing but good to her. Straight. "Straight!"

Why was my search for happiness always on a road going the wrong way? Was it me?

I stared at my reflection, and it shook me. My eyes I didn't recognize. They were empty. If the eyes were the window to the soul, then mine abandoned me. And there was an ache inside of me like I'd never experienced before. I felt as if I were being ripped apart, and it was then that I realized just how deeply I'd fallen in love with Maxine. If I weren't, this day, this time, would have never been able to hurt me. I'd taken a risk, allowing myself to put aside my bitterness, my doubts about women and relationships, and let her into my life. And this was what she did to me.

My thoughts began to shift, then. All kinds of old wive's tales and quotes from the Bible circled around in my head. The one that stuck was something like, The Lord gives and He takes away.

Maybe it was the reverse, I thought suddenly. Maybe I was getting some sort of chance to get something back that had been taken from me. I didn't know. I wasn't sure what I was thinking.

I didn't want to lose her. I was coming to grips with that. Slowly the idea formed and took root. But how could I fit into her life now—did she even want me there? A bigger question was, why was she even going through with this pregnancy when she knew there was no chance for her and this guy? Or maybe she thought there was. Karen hadn't seemed to have a problem making her decision, and she had claimed to love me. Was Maxine still in love with Quinn?

Was she?

I looked up. My reflection was staring back at me, but something inside was beginning to stir. I could almost see the questions in my eyes. I took a longer look. The only person who had the answers was Maxine. And I had to be able to handle whatever those answers were.

When I came out of the bathroom, Maxine was sitting on the couch. She looked up when I stepped into the room, then turned away. I didn't know what that meant, but I did know we had to talk. I took a deep breath, stuck my hands in my pants pockets, and took a chance.

"Do you still love him, Maxine? I need to know that before I say anything else."

She stared at me for a long moment, really seeming to weigh the gravity of the question, and how little or how much she was going to hurt me with her answer.

"All I know for sure, Taylor, is that I love this baby I'm carrying. Quinten made his choice, and I made mine." She touched her flat stomach. "This child was conceived in love. I could have chosen to do something entirely different—not gone through with it. I didn't. This is my child, someone I helped to create. I couldn't live with myself if I were the cause of it not having the chance to be."

I crossed the room and sat beside her. Tentatively I slid my arm around her shoulder and pulled her close, waited to feel how her body would respond to my touch. By degrees I felt her yield to my embrace, and a sense of hope lifted my battered spirit. And I knew what I must do. The step I was about to take would change her life and mine, and that of the child she carried, but I couldn't do anything else. This was my second chance.

It's not often that you get a second chance at life. The chance to get it right the next go–round. Now I did. I had the opportunity to prove to myself that I could give love unselfishly and be worthy of it in return. The chance to be strong, needed, and still be accepted as a man who cared deeply and know that it was okay.

If I took this step there was no turning back. I, we, had the chance to show a child what it was to have two people who loved each other, who would devote themselves to that child's happiness—something I never had. And my hope was that in giving I would somehow find that little boy inside of me that had been lost. I never knew what he was like, and I wanted to experience it—with Maxine. That joy.

I stood and began to pace. I needed some distance between us so I could say what needed to be said without the persuasion of the feel of her in my arms.

"If you let me, Maxine . . . I want to be here for you. Unless you have someone else who—"

"No. There's no one. But . . . I can't ask you to put

yourself out like that. This isn't your problem. It's mine. I appreciate you're wanting to do that. Really. But—''

"You're not asking me. I want to. But I need to say this to you." I paused a moment to gather my thoughts around me. "I feel as if I've been shredded. Everything from rage to betrayal to hurt has been battling in my head. I started to just walk out and keep going. There was a part of me that said, 'you don't need this in your life.' And maybe I don't."

I saw her flinch, but kept my distance, my balance.

"But I need you. And with you comes the whole package." I walked a bit closer, looked her in her eyes, and bent down in front of her. "As long as I know you feel the same way we can deal with anything—make a new start from today. Us *and* the baby. Putting our pasts behind us. It's going to take work—a lot of it—and honesty that will be painful at times, and tested."

She lowered her head and sucked on her bottom lip. "I should have told you from the beginning. I shouldn't have let you get involved with me. But I started to really feel for you, even knowing the circumstances. I guess I wanted to be cared about just for a while. You know— pretend that everything was all right." Her voice cracked. "But that wasn't fair to you. And I'm sorry, Taylor. Really . . . sorry."

A tear slid down her cheek and dropped on my wrist. It was hot, and seemed to seep into my pores—just as she had the moment I met her.

"You *are* cared about, Maxine. Don't you know that?"

She looked up at me, her eyes glistening. I saw her throat moving up and down as if she were struggling for air.

"But you have to tell me what you want, if you want me in your life. If you do, I'll be there. No ties. No pressure. No promises. But I'll be there."

"Are you sure?"

I nodded. "Yes. I'm sure." All I knew at that moment, holding her, sensing her fear and loneliness, was that I didn't want to be without her. Whatever it took. Whatever that meant.

"How do we do this?" she asked.

"One day at a time."

She pressed her head on my chest, and I felt her body shudder against me. I just shut my eyes and held her, and the warmest sensation filled me. I was being given the opportunity to make a difference in someone's life, and maybe even make up for the one that was lost.

It was then that I finally understood. Karen didn't give up our baby because of me, but because of her—what she was unwilling to do, the responsibility it would have taken, and the commitment. My background, or lack of one, was a convenient excuse. A way out. Maxine was an entirely different woman, willing to risk everything for the life she carried. She didn't want a way out. That was special and sacred.

For so long I'd blamed myself for what Karen had done, believing that *I* wasn't good enough. Maybe a part of me still felt that way. But with Maxine I had the chance to change that. I hoped. . . .

Laden with memories of that time, I looked up, momentarily dazed, feeling as if I was coming to, emerging out of a deep sleep.

"So what are you gonna do, man? CJ" asked grounding me in the present.

"I was hoping it would be cool if I camped out at your crib for a few days. Just until I think through some things."

He clasped my shoulder. "Hey, whatever," CJ said. "You know it's not a problem. Whenever you want to kick it, I'm here."

I nodded. "Thanks, Man."

"You need to go home, get some stuff?"

I blew out a long breath. "No. Everything I need is in my car. Stopped home at lunchtime."

What I really needed was Maxine, and she was on her way to see our son's father.

MAXINE

FIVE

Every Beat of My Heart

Quiet.

The moment I set foot in the house, I knew.

The silence pounded. The only sound was the echo of the pulse beat in my ears. The vibrating stillness took on dimensions of its own. A life of nothingness now filled my home, once overflowing with the beat of tomorrow.

Room after room, the smell of loss entered my nostrils, choked me with its unmistakable odor of emptiness.

Blurred the visions became, mixing colors and patterns until it all was everything and nothing.

Ty was gone.

Only the remnants of undesirables remained in the closet, where his suits had once hung, now picked over like a bargain basement sale.

Everywhere I turned there were glimmers of him, caught in my peripheral vision like a phantasm on the moors in an old English movie—there, but not. His scent lingered in the air, tricking my heart into believing that he was surrounding me in the comfort of his solid presence—a presence he'd promised me he'd always be. But it wasn't true, and the truth opened the old wounds and feelings of loss, feelings of being cast aside, feelings of uncertainty.

What could I do now but move forward? To turn back would not recover the one instant in time when this moment would not have existed. You couldn't go back.

I'd felt this before. This hole in my spirit. I felt it when Lacy died, when I broke off my engagement to Andre and gave his ring back, when Quinn walked out the door. Humph. Quinn said he'd needed to face me and tell me that he was returning to Nikita. He couldn't take the easy way out by simply walking away without explaining, even as much as it hurt. And as painful as that moment was, everything we'd ever meant to each other would have been nullified if we had not *shared* in the pain of that parting.

I couldn't take the easy way out either.

What would be easy was to find Ty—tell him to come home, love me, be with me, forgive me for hurting him. I had to deal with the consequences of my choices, though. I had to unmask what really hid in my heart once and for all in order for me to be whole for myself, my son and Taylor. If I left this undone, these loose ends untied, I would always have doubts, not about Quinn, but about Taylor and I. It is the truth that will test the strength of our survival as a couple.

Ty made his choice when he decided he didn't want to see the final act. I couldn't blame him. He was just as afraid as I was, afraid of what I would discover. But even in his fear, was the strength of his convictions. He did what he felt he must do, and so must I.

In the morning I would fly to New York. I would face the father of my child for the first time in three years. Taylor and I *would* work it out when I returned. One way or another.

* * *

"Taylor didn't come home last night?" Marva asked the next day as we drove to the airport.

I peeked at the back seat. Jamel was fast asleep. "No."

"No phone call?"

"Nothing." I folded my arms to keep Marva from seeing my shaking hands.

"Aren't you worried?"

"Taylor is a grown man, Marva. I'm sure he knew what he was doing when he packed his bags. He's probably at CJ's."

I caught her looking at me from the corner of her eye, and hoped she didn't notice the circles under mine. My dreams were haunted with dark shadows and voices with no faces, asking questions I couldn't answer. I turned so many times during my restless night, seeking the warmth and security of Taylor's arms, but he wasn't there.

"Don't you want to call and see if he's home? Say good–bye?"

"It's not going to change anything. Just make it harder." What I feared most was that he'd tell me not to go—that if I loved him I would stay—and that I wouldn't be able to do what he asked."

"Why, Maxine? Not talking is what got you and Ty into this mess in the first place."

"I tried to talk to him. He didn't want to listen."

"Really?"

Her sarcasm attached itself to me, and I couldn't shake it off even when I snatched a look in her direction. "Yes. Really."

"Hmm."

"What's that supposed to mean?"

"You have a lot of thinking to do, Max. Some real soul searching. You need to ask yourself why you're doing this, why you're willing to jeopardize your entire life for Quinten

Parker—again. *Again,* Maxine. Why you can't be honest with Taylor. But I think you know the answers to that—you aren't being honest with yourself.

"You've made some tough decisions, life altering decisions, and stuck by them. You're not a quitter, and you don't let the worst get you down. But when you get to New York and you see Quinn again, you need to search your soul like you've never done before."

I lowered my head, momentarily ashamed at having attempted to take my fears and frustrations out on her. I knew that at the root of her scolding and probing she had my best interests at heart.

"I'm sorry," I whispered. "You're right."

She turned to me and smiled. "I know."

Moments later we pulled into the departure area and came to a stop behind a minivan full of Chinese tourists. I could tell because they all had cameras dangling from their necks. It almost made me smile.

Jamel whined for a moment, his sleep disturbed by the sudden lack of motion, rubbed his eyes, and sat up. "Mommy."

I got out of the car, opened his door, and scooped him out.

"Where we go?" he asked.

I kissed the top of his head. "Mommy has to take a short trip on the airplane." I pointed toward the clouds, watching his dark eyes follow the line of my finger. "Remember, I told you? I'll be back tomorrow, sweetness."

He wrapped his arms around my neck. "I wanna go wit you."

I gave him a squeeze. "Not this time, darling. Mommy has some important things to do. You're going to stay with Auntie Marva until I get back."

Marva eased up alongside of us and ran her hands across his head of tight curls.

"We'll have fun, Mel–Mel," she promised, using her

pet name for him, making him blush and bury his face in my hair.

"Where's my daddy?" he mumbled.

Marva and I cut quick, unsteady looks at each other. Gently she extricated him from my arms.

"Your dad has some things to do, too, Mel," she answered, her tone a mixture of firmness and love.

It always amazed me how good she was with Jamel, with children in general. I'd seen her interact with kids who came into the agency with their parents. She had a natural maternal instinct. The shame of it was, she couldn't have children of her own.

I remember when she'd confided that to me, and the painful revelation cemented our friendship even more. . . .

We'd been sitting in my garden, and I'd just dried up my tears after blurting out that I was pregnant with Quinn's child, my desire to keep it, and my uncertainty about my future and the rightness of it all.

For a while neither of us spoke. She simply sat there, sipping her lemonade and looking out toward the Golden Gate Bridge. And then she slowly began to talk.

"I was scared and desperate," she began, her voice sounding as if it were traveling over the miles of time. "I was seventeen—two months before graduation—and pregnant. All I knew was that I had to walk onto that platform, get my diploma, make my folks proud, and move on to college."

"Did you . . . love him?"

A sad smile flickered across her mouth like a lightbulb getting ready to blow out.

"I thought I did. But who knows about love, its magnitude and consequences, at seventeen?" She laughed shortly and put her glass down on the white, cast-iron table. Leaning back against the green-and-white striped canvas lounge chair, she looked out across the manicured hedges. "I certainly didn't know what love really meant.

My concern was not about whether I was in love but about the wrath and disappointment of my parents, the stigma that would invariably be stamped on my chest in the exclusive, above reproach neighborhood in which I lived. Not to mention the four year scholarship to Smith that I'd lose if I went through with it. Love, *ha.* As much as I may have loved him, it was overpowered by the things that I believed counted.''

She leaned forward and retrieved her glass, taking a long, slow swallow. She held the glass slightly away from her lips as if the next words she uttered could be dropped inside and then swallowed back down, returning to that dark place in all of us where secrets dwell.

"So I did the only thing I could. I found someone who could make my troubles go away—for a price, of course. And I, being weaned on the belief that money can buy you anything you want—paid the price."

I saw her eyes glisten and brim with water as she bit down on her trembling bottom lip, struggling for control.

Her voice was choked, tight, when she continued. "An hour after I walked into that back room office I left there believing that my future had been returned to me for six hundred dollars. The truth—that I'd left my future in a heap of bloodstained sheets on the floor—was revealed to me a week later when I wound up in the hospital, closer to death than I am sitting next to you.

"The doctors fixed me up, though. Removed everything that had been damaged. 'You should have a perfectly normal life,' they said, 'but unfortunately you won't be able to have children.' "

I reached for her hand, which she put into mine as I watched the tears finally slide down her cheeks.

"I didn't tell you that to force you to make a choice, or a decision." She sniffed and wiped away her tears with her free hand. "I just want you to see that sometimes in life what we think is important isn't, and we make bad choices.

I learned. The hard way. It's not about doing things to please others or to make life easy, but what you in your heart feel to be the right thing. That's why when Brent came into my life, I knew come hell or high water I was going to go against every iota of everything I'd been born and bred on to have him.''

She squeezed my hand. "Do what's in your heart, Maxine. Be honest with yourself about your choices, and your reasons why. That's all.''

Those words stayed with me, rising up now more than ever as I kissed my son and my dearest friend one more time and walked toward the gates.

Even as the 747 soared across the bay and up into the heavens, leaving behind things familiar and comfortable, I knew I couldn't fly away from the truth. Staring out the window, I watched the clouds dance by. A huge metal bird flying in the sky went against everything that made sense, yet it existed. It happened every day. The inexplicable magic of flight would never be understood or explained by me, and in that moment I realized that until I truly understood my feelings for Quinn I would never be able to explain them to Taylor, or to myself.

Taylor. What must he be thinking—feeling? It was all so unfair. He'd never been anything but straight with me, from the moment he'd made the decision to be a part of my life.

And I'd given into his will, his determination to make it work. I'd pushed back whatever it was I thought I still felt for Quinn and allowed Taylor's love to take its place. But had I really? That was the question that frightened me, that stood now as the wall between me and Taylor. And what of the most precious piece of this puzzle—Jamel? Above all things, he must be my first concern.

"Would you like to watch the movie?" the stewardess asked, displaying a plastic bag containing a set of headphones.

Looking up at her, seeing her practiced smile and congenial manner, I suddenly saw how much of life is all pretense. Pretending things are what they aren't just to keep peace, to make the day–to–day easy, to be safe from the things we don't want to deal with. We do what is comfortable, slipping into a state of complacency until life in all its glory strikes.

I returned her smile. "No thank you. I have a lot of thinking to do."

I adjusted my seat and leaned back, momentarily shutting my eyes. Just contemplating what I would face within the next hours escalated the shifting in my stomach. I tried to rest, but my spiraling thoughts wouldn't let me.

I opened my eyes, looking around at the collection of passengers, playing a game with myself by trying to figure out their lives, in the vain hope that it would distract me from my own.

Businessmen with laptops, college students with open textbooks perhaps on their way back to school from short vacations, couples who sat close whispering tender words to each other, the single man or woman quietly reading airline publications to occupy their time until they met their loved ones filled the rows. But what caught and held my attention was a family seated across from me and a row ahead. The little girl, who couldn't have been more than five was proudly displaying a drawing.

The picture, all stick figures, were of a man, a woman and a little girl all holding hands in front of a house. I could almost feel the parents' pride and joy at what their child had created. The little girl's dad oohed and ahhed and ruffled her hair. The mother squeezed her tightly and told her how wonderful the drawing was, and how wonderful she was.

"That's us," the man said to his daughter. "One big happy family."

"Yep," the little girl responded.

"And who's daddy's favorite girl?"

"Me!" she squealed as he tickled her stomach.

Something deep in mine knotted. How often had I wanted that same adoration and unflinching love showered on me by my father?

I remember one evening my father had just gotten in from work. He worked for a meat packing company and came in every evening weary and silent. I'd just gotten my fifth grade report card—straight 'A's' except in math where I got a 'C', but I was so proud and couldn't wait to show my daddy.

I ran to him the moment he came through the door.

"Daddy, Daddy look," I sang proudly, holding up my report card for him to see.

He took it from my hand, barely acknowledging me, giving the pale blue card a cursory glance.

"What's this 'C'? In math?" he boomed, turning dark eyes on me.

My heart began to hammer. I couldn't find words.

"I—"

"Answer me. You can do better than this, Maxine. You obviously got too much free time. Not studying like you're supposed to. How do you expect to get anywhere in the world with 'C's?"

He handed the card back to me. "Go on up to your room. Your mother and I will think of an appropriate punishment."

My eyes filled and my throat knotted in pain. I turned, feeling small, my achievements worthless. Of all I'd accomplished, all he could see was what I didn't do, not what I'd done.

Hmm. It was always like that. No matter what I did: perform in a school play, pass a test, join cheerleaders, clean the house, cook, wash. It didn't much matter. Richard Sherman always knew I could do better. On rare occasions he would give me a hug or a smile when I'd exceeded even my own expectations. I lived for those moments.

As I grew older I began to believe that I had to work for love and affection from a man. That I had to be the giving one, the one who was willing to go the extra mile in order to receive anything in return. Or I'd go to the opposite extreme and do nothing for fear of losing, of being hurt.

During my teen years and early adulthood, Quinn fit the bill on both levels. Although he was never mean or cold, there was a distance about him which dredged up all the unspoken emotions I had that were unresolved with my dad. Quinn's redeeming quality was that there was a part of him that could truly care. And because I saw that kernel, that little unnoticed girl in me wanted to make it grow, but the push-pull in me couldn't move to make it happen, even at the expense of my relationship with Andre Martin.

Andre, or Dre as I called him, was really a great guy, and I know he truly loved me. I really thought that if I immersed myself into that relationship, I could finally cleanse myself of this unseen power Quinten Parker had over my life. I was wrong. And I'd hurt Andre as a result. Our parting was painful, but Dre made me realize something I'd ignored for far too long. I had to face what was really inside me if I ever hoped to be truly happy.

Dre and I got engaged on Christmas Eve. At first I was hesitant to take the ring, but I knew I was getting a good man, a man who loved me. I convinced myself that I would make it work, that I'd put all my energies into the two of us.

But as time passed, and Dre kept pressing me for a wedding date, and I kept avoiding it, there was no way either of us could have gotten around the final day.

"Max, we need to talk," Dre said, sitting on the edge of my bed.

I stretched and turned on my side, totally satisfied from our hours-plus of much needed sex.

"About what?" I asked.

"About us."

I squeezed my eyes shut for a hot minute, took a breath and sat up, pulling the floral patterned sheet up to cover my breasts.

"I'm listening."

He turned, angling his body to face me. "You've been wearing that ring for six months, Max. And every time I mention setting a date, you go into your bag of excuses, why, 'Now is not a good time to discuss it.' Now. Tonight is the time, Max. I get the feeling that marrying me is not really what you want to do."

My throat tightened when I looked into his Michael Jordan look-alike face. He loved me. Really loved me. And as much as I'd tried, I didn't feel the same way.

"Dre, I—"

He held up his hand. "Don't. Don't give me a long story and try to save my feelings. Just answer me in one simple word, Max. Do you want to marry me, yes or no?"

I drew my knees up to my chest and lowered my head, unable to look him in the eye. "No," I mumbled into the softness of the cotton sheets.

Dre and I did remain 'friend's, though. He stayed in touch even when I moved out to San Francisco, and I was really glad to hear that he'd found someone and was getting married. Dre deserved it. He was a good man, just not the man for me. For all that Andre Martin was, he didn't fill all of the spaces in me, and what I realized over time, was that neither did Quinn.

There was a spark, a definite attraction, but there were pieces missing, that elusiveness I couldn't seem to grasp. And just as Dre wasn't the man for me, I wasn't the woman for Quinn. I was too accessible. I made *us* too easy for him. Quinn needed challenge, obstacles, a push—Nikita provided that, as much as I may be unwilling to admit. But she did. Just as Taylor filled all the spaces and provided what I needed. We fit.

That's what Dre had been trying to tell me—that until I came to grips with that—answered the things that were unresolved—what was truly in my heart, took a stand and not let indecision paralyze me—I would never be happy.

These past days resurrected all those old feelings. Feelings of neediness, dreams unfulfilled, the on-going push-pull. And with that realization came a sense of peace, because I was no longer that person and hadn't been for a while. I was a woman now, a three dimensional woman. Taylor's woman.

By the time my plane descended onto the runway of Kennedy Airport, I was bone tired. The mental exertion of wrestling with my thoughts, combined with a lack of sleep and a bumpy ride, all contributed to my exhaustion. A part of me still wanted to go back, forget the whole thing, and hope that I could patch things up with Taylor. But deep inside I had known that this day would come— if not now, then sometime in the future.

There was more to consider than simply attending the funeral for Nikita, and seeing Quinn. It was about dealing with issues I'd tried to pretend didn't exist for the past three years. That didn't make them go away. They'd only magnified over time. How would I ever be able to make Quinn understand why I handled things the way I did— why I never told him about his son? Would he understand? And where would it leave everyone in the end?

All of these questions, and more that I couldn't begin to formulate, spun around in my head as I walked through the arrival gates, seeing Val waving to me above the crowd. For a moment, seeing her familiar face, I felt a sense of ease, one which I knew was only temporary.

"Max. It's so good to see you, Girl."

She wrapped me in a hug. Wow, it felt good. It was like truly coming home. I stepped back and looked her over.

"You must be making the bucks at the law firm, Val. That suit is working."

She spun around dramatically. "Hey, with the cases that Sean and Khendra have been throwing my way, I have to look the part of the high-powered attorney."

"Listen to you, Ms. Thang," I said, planting my hand on my hip. We both laughed.

"You're looking pretty sharp yourself. That California life is doing wonders for you."

"Life's been good, Val. It really has." And I meant it.

Val nodded, then put her arm around my shoulder as we started toward the baggage claim. "I'm glad you came, Max. Really. I know it won't be easy for you. But Quinn will appreciate you coming."

I took in a long breath. "I wish it were that easy. You know. Just coming for support."

"Are you planning to tell him—about Jamel?" she asked.

"It's time."

"How does Taylor feel about that?"

"Let's say he didn't take it very well."

"Hmm. I'm sure he'll come around. He has to know it's the right thing to do, Maxine."

"Sometimes Val, right and wrong have nothing to do with the way you feel inside."

"How are *you* dealing with it?"

"I'm still trying to figure that one out," I replied, a drop of sadness in my voice. "But I will. Before I go back home, I will."

QUINN

SIX

Things Fall Apart

The knocking on the parlor floor door disturbed me. I didn't want to be disturbed. I wanted to be swallowed whole in the emptiness I felt, the guilt that slowly had begun to eat away at my spirit, eroding it, like water beating relentless against a rock, changing its shape.

That knocking again. That damned knocking wouldn't stop. The calls and the people wouldn't stop. Everyone wanted to help. Help! Didn't they realize they couldn't? That no amount of phone calls, cards, flowers, and plates of food were going to bring Nikita back to me? Nothing on this earth could do that. And nothing in heaven, either. I'd learned that years ago.

I just wanted to be left alone. Alone. Why was that so hard to understand? I took a long swallow of Jack Daniels. I think it was my fourth one for the morning. Maybe it was more. I'd lost count.

"Quinten! Quinten Parker! You open this door right this minute, or I'll use the key."

It was Mrs. Finch, my landlady and surrogate mother of sorts. She'd treated me like a son from the first day we'd met. Once I got used to her bossing me around and poking her nose in my business, I actually began to like the attention. The feeling of being treated like a man, but still being cared about like someone's child. Never really had that coming up. Even before my moms cut out Lacy and me, we pretty much took care of ourselves.

"Quinten Parker. I mean it. Open this door, right now."

I practically threw myself off the couch, knowing that if I didn't stop her she would follow through with her threat to come in anyway.

I pulled the door open, and it was clear my appearance shocked her from the look of wide-eyed surprise on her face. She turned up her narrow nose.

"You've been drinking."

"Yep."

She brushed by me and stepped into the living room. "What good do you think getting drunk is going to do?"

"None."

"Then why do it, Quinten?"

Mrs. Finch was the only one I let get away with calling me Quinten, and she knew it. "Takes the edge off, ya know?"

"It's only a temporary solution, son. After it wears off, whatever is eating at you is still there. You have to confront it and deal with it."

"Maybe I won't let it wear off." My head was spinning. I had to sit down. Gingerly, I eased back over to the couch, hoping I wasn't swaying the way the room was. I flopped down, leaned my head back, and closed my eyes. "Maybe I don't want to confront and deal with it."

"So you plan to drink yourself into oblivion?"

"Yep."

She sat down beside me and talked to me like the little boy I felt I'd become since that damned phone call from the hospital.

"I worry about you, Quinten. I know you're hurt. Devastated. But Niki wouldn't have wanted you to do this to yourself."

"How do you know what she would have wanted? Huh?" I shouted, and it sounded as if a band had gone off in my head. "Nobody knows what Nikita would have wanted. She didn't even know. All she knew for sure was that she wanted more. Just like her mommy and daddy taught her." I started laughing. It began deep in my belly, worming its way up my chest and out my throat. I couldn't stop. I began rambling and crying like a punk, over the laughter. "She wanted more for me. Always did. Thought I could do great things. She believed in me. Really believed in me. But it was hard, Mrs. Finch. Really hard to constantly keep livin' up to this ideal she had of me. But I loved her. I loved her."

I tried to pull myself up, brace my arms on my thighs. I didn't want her to see me bawling. But where could I go but deeper into this abyss that loomed before me?

Mrs. Finch put her thin arm around my shoulder and the scent of Gold Bond powder wafted to my nose, setting my stomach to spinning.

"I know you loved her, son. I know you did. That's why you have to pull yourself together. Not just for Niki, but for yourself. For the love the two of you shared."

"Everything I ever cared about been taken from me, Mrs. Finch. Everything. One by one. My mama. Lacy. Nikita."

I buried my face in my hands. I didn't give a damn anymore if she saw me crying. I didn't give a damn 'bout anything.

"Quinten, now you listen to me. You have the rest of your life ahead of you. You have your music, your writing, and people who care about you, son." She squeezed my shoulder.

I jerked away, stood up too suddenly, and nearly fell over the coffee table. I kicked it, sending the crystal vase of flowers that sat on its center crashing to the floor.

"I told Niki about that damned table being too close to the couch. I told her. She wouldn't listen. Said it looked good just where it was, and to watch my big feet."

I started laughing again, and Ms. Finch was getting kind of scared.

"Quinten, I'm going to call Nick and tell him to come over here until you pull yourself together."

"Don't call nobody. Sick of seein' people . . . askin' me if I'm all right. I ain't all right, okay? And I don't plan to be all right for a long time."

I tried to focus on the half glass of Jack that miraculously remained unharmed on the table. But I couldn't figure out which glass to pick up.

Then all of a sudden, Mrs. Finch grabbed my arm. Tight. I didn't know she was that strong. She was no bigger than a bird, but she had a grip on me that wouldn't quit.

"You get yourself upstairs. I don't want to hear any more of this craziness coming from you."

She started tugging on me, and in my state I soon realized that my six–three height and two–twenty–five weight were no match for her. I started to really freak when I imagined that if I didn't do what she said she'd tug me by the ear or whip my tail with my own belt.

Somehow I managed to stumble up the stairs with the help of a lot of pulling and threats from Mrs. Finch.

Before I realized what was happening, she'd pushed me through my bedroom, into the bathroom, and under the ice cold pellets of the shower.

When that water hit me I started hollering and cussing all at the same time, but that tiny little woman held me under that water by sheer strength of will until I started shaking and my head began to clear.

She turned off the water, wrapped two towels around my body, and helped me into my room.

"Now, get out of those wet things," she ordered, her arms folded. Determined.

"You're gonna stand there and watch me get undressed?"

She blew out a breath. "Believe me, you don't have a thing I haven't seen."

"But—"

"Shut your mouth and get out of those clothes."

I wobbled a little and tried to stare her down. It didn't do any good. She just stood there watching me tremble in the big puddle of water that was forming at my feet.

I glared at her one more time, and she started tapping her foot.

"Damn." I started pulling off my shirt.

"Told you about cussing."

"Sorry," I mumbled and unbuckled my belt.

"You get finished. I'll be back soon."

She turned and walked out, leaving the door slightly ajar. I wasn't sure if she'd left because she really didn't want to see what I had, or if she actually had something to do. In any case I was just relieved that I didn't have to stand in front of her in my birthday suit and then look her in the face tomorrow.

Tomorrow. Nikita's funeral was tomorrow. Wasn't it? They were going to close up that box and put her in the ground. Away from me for good.

Humph. Mrs. Finch was right. All the drinking in the world couldn't make that fact go away.

I sat down on the edge of the bed, wondering how I was going to get through tomorrow. Or the rest of my life. There was no one who really understood how helpless and weak I felt. No one except maybe Maxine. But she was

gone, too. Living her life up in Frisco. Hadn't talked to
Max in way too long. Not since . . . Well, I didn't want to
think about it. I know I hurt her when I told her I was
coming back to New York to be with Nikita. I didn't mean
to hurt her. Didn't want to, ya know? But what else could
I do?

I just hoped that Max found a way to understand and
forgive me. She said she did. But Max was always like that—
easy, ya know? Hoped she was happy.

Maxine had her life and I had mine—what was left of
it. But how was I going to live it without Niki? She gave
me the push I needed, even though I fought her tooth
and nail every chance I got. She was tough to be so little.
Like Mrs. Finch.

"Here, I brought you some soup."

I looked up. I hadn't heard the tiny terror come back
into the room, and I still hadn't put on any clothes.

She set the bowl of soup—chicken, I thought—on the
nightstand by the bed, then went in the linen closet in the
bathroom and brought back a towel. She draped it across
my lap.

"So you don't get a chill," she said, sounding mildly
serious, then sat down next to me. "Eat your soup, son.
It's good for you."

My stomach felt as if someone had put a spinning top
at high speed in it, and I was pretty sure that soup would
only add to the frenzy, but if I didn't do it, she'd probably
start spoon–feeding me.

With shaky hands I reached for the bowl and placed
it on my towel–covered thighs. After the first couple of
spoonfuls I actually started to feel a bit better. At least the
room was finally within the speed limit, and my stomach
began to settle down to a dance I could keep up with.

"You may not believe this," Mrs. Finch began in a soft,
thoughtful tone, "but I was young once."

We turned toward each other and smiled.

"When I was twenty–two I met John. As soon as I laid eyes on that man I knew he was the man I was going to marry. And I did."

In all the years I'd known Mrs. Finch, lived in her house, I'd never thought of her as ever being married. She never talked about herself, or ever mentioned a husband. Maybe I should have known—if I hadn't been so wrapped up in my own life—that someone as giving as Mrs. Finch had to have somebody who cared about her in return.

"We shared thirty wonderful years together. Some not so wonderful," she amended. "There were some rough spots, differences of opinions. But for the most part they were good years. Our biggest downfall was working too hard, not taking enough time for each other, too busy trying to build that nest egg. John worked sometimes eighteen hours a day so that he could give me what he thought I needed and deserved.

"Then, one Saturday afternoon in July he was sitting in his favorite chair by the window reading the sports section of the *Daily News*—and he died. Just like that." She snapped her skinny fingers for emphasis.

"I'm . . . sorry."

She waved her hand in dismissal. "That was nearly twenty years ago."

She was quiet for a moment, and I wondered if that was the whole story, and why she'd told me in the first place.

"For years after his death," she began again, "I blamed myself. Some days my guilt weighed me down so heavy I couldn't get out of my bed. I felt like if I'd just spoken up, told him to slow down, stood my ground, he wouldn't have worked so hard and he wouldn't have died. But I had to let it go. The guilt. Just like *you're* going to have to let it go, or it will eat you alive. You can't go back and make it right. You must move forward and make the very best life you can."

"You make it sound so easy. Like all I have to do is say

some magic words and this feelin' is gonna go away. It won't. I know it. Not this time."

I lowered my head, feeling another wave of sorrow wash over me, making my head light and my blood run hot and cold.

"What do you mean, not this time, Quinten?"

"Can't talk about it." I shook my head. "Can't."

She put her hand on the back of my neck and gently rubbed it. I felt the knots of tension loosen beneath her fingertips. For a few seconds I allowed the sensation of ease to become a part of me, push the tightness away. My eyes drifted shut.

Niki did that a lot. She possessed magic fingers. Always knew when things were closing in on me, even when what made me crazed was something she'd done.

Mrs. Finch took the bowl of soup off my lap and put it back on the nightstand.

I glanced at her, then looked away.

"I'm listening, Quinten. It's long past time that you talked about what's been in your heart—and on your conscience."

I didn't see how talking was going to change anything, how it would make this deadness inside get filled up with life again.

"It couldn't have been easy for the two of you . . . coming from different worlds and all," she said, her tone taking on a storytelling quality, relaxing me. "Must have been hard at times."

I nodded. "Yeah. It was. Harder than I thought it would be. I guess I figured I'd be who I was and she'd be herself, and somehow it would just work out. But we were always at odds about one thing or the other."

"*Hmmm.* It can be that way when you have two strong—willed people under the same roof."

I smiled a little. "No doubt. Niki was strong all right—determined, ya know? Once she set her mind to somethin', that was it. But sometimes . . . I felt like I was losin' myself, givin' up a part of me to make her happy, keep the peace.''

"When you love someone, Quinten, you make sacrifices, concessions. It's all part of being a couple."

"But it should work both ways, ya know? Not always one person expectin', expectin' and the other one givin'. We didn't know anything about being a couple. That's the one thing we never figured out. Up until I met Nikita, I'd never spent any real time with a woman. They didn't expect me to, and I didn't want to. That's just the way it was. But Niki, ha, she wasn't going for that. Only problem was, she was just as green in this relationship thing as I was. And it was a struggle, every day."

"That's what you feel happened with you and Nikita?"

I wrapped the towel around my waist, stood and began pacing the floor. I knew it was the liquor that was pushing the words out of my mouth. True confession wasn't my style. But maybe I needed to get it out. I crossed the room.

"It ain't right to feel this anger toward her, Mrs. Finch, but I do. She never let up. Never. What I wanted didn't matter. It wasn't in the plan—her plan. That's . . . that's what we fought about . . . the day she—I think that if I hadn't said what I did, if I'd just let it go and not given her an ultimatum, she would've been thinkin' clearly. She would've seen . . . Damn. I can't do this."

I turned toward the window and stared out at the garden that Niki and I had worked on together. It was bursting with color and life. It made me smile for a minute, and then I felt myself choking up again, that weakness coming over me, turning me into the kind of man I'd never accept being—soft, vulnerable.

How many nights had I stayed awake staring at the ceiling, thinking that I was changing? That the code I'd lived by for all my life—"Never let them see how you feel"— was losing ground. Nikita made me feel, forced me to deal with my emotions. Made me say the things on my mind, and in my heart, even when I didn't want to—even when I felt that it would make me less of a man.

"But above all else, you loved each other, Quinten. I could see it," she said, cutting off my thoughts.

I pushed out a long breath. "But there was always a battle going on inside me, Mrs. Finch, ya know? All I'd ever known was the street, the hustle, the will to survive. After my sister, Lacy, was killed, all my reason for doing anything—even getting up in the morning—seemed to die with her. For a long time I blamed myself. Some days I still do, but I found a way to handle it. If only I'd listened to her about getting out of the 'hood, movin' someplace decent where we didn't have to worry about drive–bys, break–ins and drug busts. That's all she wanted for the both of us. But I didn't listen. I didn't. That was my world. All I knew. Maybe even a part of me was scared of that something else, that something different."

"There's no way you could have known what was going to happen to your sister, Quinten. It was a tragic, horrible accident—"

"But don't you see, if I'd listened, worked with her to get out, she'd still be alive. That's why I tried so hard with Niki. I thought, believed, I was given a second chance to do the right thing, to fill my sister's dream for me. I promised myself that I would listen, that Niki saw the bigger picture, that I wouldn't fight her on her master plan for our life, because if I did, I'd lose her, too. And the one time that I did—I lost her.

"I thought I could somehow make amends for Lacy's death, that it wouldn't have been for nothin'. But I started to lose a piece of myself day by day, 'til I couldn't tell me from Niki. And it made me crazy inside, made me ache 'til I wanted to scream. 'Til I wouldn't come home at night 'cause I needed to hold onto the pieces of myself that kept fallin' away from me, like on a crumbling brick building."

I blinked, and the garden came back into focus, shutting

out the room and Mrs. Finch. I could almost see the image of Niki in her overalls, on her hands and knees tending to the flowers—humming some song, way off beat 'cause she couldn't hold a note—and something inside of me twisted in pain.

"She'd been working in the garden . . . that morning. She did that a lot over the past months when she had something on her mind. Said it eased her, helped her to think.

That morning she said, "You know how Amy, my folks' housekeeper, taught me all about gardening? How she was always so good to me, like a real mother? Sometimes, when I was little, I wished she was my mother; did I tell you that? I know that's a terrible thing to say, but it's true. You know how my mother resented me, always did—that color thing of hers, how she didn't want anything in her life to remind her that she was black—including me."

She focused her gaze on the pile of earth she was turning, letting it spill through her gloved hands.

I could almost understand why my mama left us the way she did. It was more of a survival thing for her. She couldn't handle the responsibility of raising two kids on her own. She'd never had a life, having us when she was only seventeen. That I'd come to grips with over the years. That was something concrete. But this . . . I never understood it.

"My mother figured she'd have a light, bright baby," Niki said. "A child who would confirm her belief that she was of substance, that she belonged. You know that every time she looked at me, she saw her own failure. You saw how she acted."

She tossed a pile of dirt to the side with a tiny shovel and let out this sigh. "So Amy became my mom, of sorts. You know how she talked to me, listened to me, scolded me. If I hadn't had her, I don't know what I would have done."

"Is that why you try so hard, Niki—to prove somethin' to your folks?"

She shrugged. "Maybe. Maybe to myself."

She looked up at me, then, with that expression she gave me sometimes that seemed to say I could make everything right with her world. When she did that, when I saw that sparkle in her eyes, the love she had for me that seemed to make her glow, I felt as if I *could* do anything. Anything she wanted.

"Do you feel you have to prove somethin' to me, too?" I asked her.

"Yes. I do. Every day. I have to prove to you that you didn't make a mistake by marrying me. That just because we grew up in two different worlds, doesn't mean that it can't work. I have to prove to you that I can be a part of your world, and you a part of mine." She looked away. "Whatever it takes."

"But we have everything, Niki. What else is there to prove? Your publishing company is doing well. My music is taking off. I know my next book is going to be off the hook. And the Lacy Parker Foundation is solid." I sat down beside her, forgetting about my clothes, which I'd just gotten out of the cleaners. I took her hand. "The only thing missing is a baby. I want a family. That would make everything complete, Niki."

"We *are* a family," she said in that tight voice, set for battle, pulling her hand away. "We talked about this before, Quinn. It's not time."

"When will it be time? We've been married for almost three years already. Whenever I bring it up you have a reason why not. *We don't have enough money. You have a big project coming up. I'm on tour. You're not ready.*"

"I want everything to be right with us, Quinn."

"Everything like what?"

"Like us really working as a team. Understanding each other. You coming home at night, and me not having to worry about where you are. Saving enough money, and making sure our futures are secure.''

"That's bull, and you know it.''

"That's your answer to everything you don't agree with.'' She jammed the little shovel into the dirt.

"Oh. So it's my fault, as usual. I bend over backwards for you, Nikita. You wanted me to go back to school, so I did. You wanted me to write, so I did. You wanted me to cut loose some of my friends, and I did. But it's never enough. Maybe if I had someone to come home to at night that wanted *me* there and not some remake, I'd be here more often. Ever think of that? Maybe if I could put my feet up on my own damned table and not have to hear you complain about it, I'd sit around more often. You ever ask yourself why I left you in the first place? Why I just took off?''

"Because you couldn't handle it,'' she snapped. "You couldn't deal with a woman who wouldn't allow you to be less than you could be. Who wanted more for you than being some street thug for the rest of your life. So you went running off to Maxine.''

The anger, the venom, the pain in her voice stung me. For a moment, I couldn't say anything.

Since I'd come back, told her she was the one I wanted to be with, the one I loved, we'd never spoken about those years we were apart. I never talked to her about Max, and she never asked. It was a part of our lives that was a closed case, I thought.

I was livid. "So that's what you've been thinkin' all this time, that it was all about me runnin' to Maxine? She wasn't the reason why I left you. *You* were the reason why I left you. If I hadn't, there wouldn't have been anything left of me to give to anyone. You were eating me alive, Nikita.''

"Then why did you marry me? Why?''

"I could ask you the same question. If that's how you

felt, have been feelin' all these years, why did you marry me?"

"Because I worked for it," she said from between her teeth. "From the moment you walked in *Rhythms* and sat down next to me, I worked for it."

It took a minute for what she was saying to settle, and then it hit me so hard I felt the air get stuck in my chest. "So this whole thing with us was just a test, a job, another challenge, just to see if you could, because you felt that you deserved it? Is that what you're sayin'? Deserved it! What am I, some damn prize that you can pull out like a trophy and trot around whenever the mood hits you? You're a real piece of work, Nikita. Everybody warned me about you from day one—Ms. Uptown Girl."

I heard the nastiness, the poison, that coated my words, and I didn't care. I was almost enjoying the anguished expression on her face. I wanted to hurt her. Make her feel as bottomless as I did.

"They told me you were just out to reach the top, and wouldn't care who you stepped on in the process. Guess that included me, too. But hey, I played the game. Where's my prize—you?"

I stood and headed for the door. Knew I had to get away before things got worse.

"Quinn. Wait. You don't understand. That's not what I meant."

"Hey. No need to explain. I'm not as dumb as I appear." I walked back into the house, not giving a damn that I was tracking dirt all over the floors she'd just polished. Too bad.

"So is this how it's going to be?" she shouted to my back, coming into the house behind me. "You're just going to walk out, not listen? That's part of the problem, Quinn."

I ignored her, pulled my jacket from the hook in the hall, and grabbed my car keys from the antique table she'd spent a small fortune on.

"Yeah, well the other part of the problem is leavin'." I slammed the door behind me and took off.

Not sure how long I drove around, but when I looked up I was back in my old neighborhood. Funny, that always seemed to happen when Niki and I had a fight. Not that we fought a lot, but enough, too much for me. And the battles were becoming more intense, even vicious.

I'd been so used to having my own space, running my own life, it was hard to adjust to someone else being in my life, caring about what I did. Coming up, the fellas would always say a man was whipped if he tripped all over himself doing everything his woman wanted. He was soft. I didn't know anything about being a part of a "unit", as Niki said. I tried as best I could, without giving everything up in the process, but she wanted it all. Not just my heart, which she had, but my soul.

I remember one time, I'd come home from a night of hanging out. I'd let the time get away from me, and I couldn't let my boys know I had to run home. I figured she'd be asleep when I got there. She wasn't. She was sitting up waiting for me. I guess we'd been married about two months at the time. Man, no sooner than my foot crossed the door, she was on me.

"I've been waiting for you for hours, Quinn. It's three o'clock in the morning. Where have you been?"

Her whole tone, the way she was standing and the 'you'd better give me an answer' look in her eyes immediately put me on the defensive.

"Look, Niki, don't start, okay? I'm tired."

"You don't think *I'm* tired? Tired of worrying about where you are, if something happened to you? Why didn't you call?"

"I didn't think I needed to, Nikita. I'm a grown man. When are you going to get that through your head?"

"And when are you going to get it through *your* head

that it's not all about you? That I'm your wife now, not some girlfriend you come to visit when you have the time."

I pulled off my shirt and tossed it on the chair. "We've had this conversation before. I don't want to hear it. I'm home, okay? If you were worried, I'm sorry. End of story. I'll remember to call next time."

"It's not that simple, Quinn."

I sat on the side of the bed and pulled off my shoes. "Why not? That's what you want, isn't it?"

She didn't answer, which was fine with me. She just got into bed and turned off the light.

I took a quick shower to get the scent of smoke off me and got in bed next to her. She kept her back turned, but I knew she wasn't asleep. I could tell by the way she was breathing. I turned on my side and put my arm around her waist, kissed the back of her neck. She tried to squirm away, but I hugged her tighter.

"Where you goin'?" I kissed her again. "I'm sorry, Baby. Really. I didn't mean for you to worry." I eased my hand up until it cupped her breast. I felt her body tense for an instant and then relax, that all too familiar sigh slip past her lips. "Forgive me?" I inched closer and I felt her move against me.

"It's just that I do worry," she whispered as my touch grew more aggressive. Her body shuddered in that way that made me crazy with need.

"I don't mean to make you worry." I turned her on her back and she looked up at me, all soft and sweet. I pushed her short gown up above her hips, and touched the folds between her thighs until she was wet and trembling. I eased her legs apart with a brush of my thigh, bracing my weight above her on my arms.

She kissed me, gentle and tender, running her fingers through my hair, while she raised her hips until I found her hot center. And when I slipped inside and felt her tighten around me, my head spun, my insides filled with heat, and all I could think about was making her happy, doing the right thing, whatever it took.

"I love you, Quinn."

"I know, Baby. I know."

And, just as always, making love with Niki, having her love me back, made everything seem possible. . . .

I wasn't always at the root of our problems. I mean, Nikita had a way about her, too. Growing up as an only child and having everything anyone could want made her selfish sometimes. She was like a kid who'd just broken open a piggy bank and was let loose in the toy store. Whatever she saw that struck her fancy, she had to have.

Now, I don't have a problem with having nice things. I always dug a fly crib, the best clothes, a decent ride. But I always had to work for everything. Struggle for it. So possessions mean something to me. Niki wasn't like that.

I'd come home from being on tour with my new CD, and I thought I'd walked into the wrong crib. She'd bought a whole new living room set and new drapes, rearranged all my books and tapes, and moved the piano from the spot it had been in since I moved there—not to mention hiring a new housekeeper, who was busy dusting a brand new dining room table that looked like it could seat twenty. Everything new.

I dropped my bags on the living room floor, and the woman jumped and turned toward me.

"Who the hell are you?"

She straightened and began twisting the dustrag in her hands. "Brenda Williams. Mrs. Parker hired me. This is my first day."

"Hired you to do what?"

"Clean. Do laundry. Run errands."

She looked so scared that I almost laughed, but it wasn't funny. "Where's my wife?"

"Upstairs. I think."

"Don't touch another thing. You can leave now. Your check is in the mail."

I headed upstairs.

"Nikita!"

She pulled open the bedroom door at the top of the stairs. "Quinn! You're back."

She came rushing out of the door and into my arms, locking her lips with mine. And when I felt her, held her, absorbed her happiness, I almost forgot why I'd been so upset. Nikita had that kind of power over me sometimes. Scared me.

"Ooh, Baby I'm glad you're home. I missed you," she whispered against my mouth. She took my hand. "Come inside and let me show you how much."

"Nikita—"

"Don't talk," she cooed. "We have plenty of time for talking later."

We went into our room, shut the door, and didn't surface for two hours.

"We need to talk, Niki," I said after, pulling on a pair of faded jeans and a T–shirt.

"Sure. About your trip? How was it?" She leaned back against the pillows and pulled the sheet up to her waist.

"It's not about the trip. It's about what you've been doing since I've been gone. Where's all my stuff? Why did you buy all those things without talking to me about it first? And what the hell do we need with a cleaning woman?"

She smiled. "I thought it was time we had some new furniture. You've had that couch and chair since you lived up in Harlem. We're married now. We need our own things. Some things that belong to both of us. And as for Brenda . . . we work too hard to have to worry about cleaning and shopping. She only comes twice a week."

She said all this as if it were no big deal, as if all the money she'd spent grew on the tree in the backyard.

"What makes you think I wanted new furniture? Maybe

I liked what we had. And this isn't Mama and Daddy's Long Island digs so that we need a cleaning woman, Nikita.''

"What are you trying to say, that I'm acting like my mother and father?''

"I'm saying you're acting as if what we had wasn't good enough for you, and I'm saying you're acting as if my opinion in all this doesn't matter. That's what I'm saying.''

"That's ridiculous.'' She pulled the sheet up to her chin.

"Nikita, you're used to having what you want when you want it. It's that simple. I'm in this, too. Now I can't do much about the furniture. But I sent Brenda on her way. She won't be back.''

"But—''

"I'm not tryin' to hear it. I'll be back later.''

"Where are you going?''

"Out.''

Didn't have too much more trouble like that, but there were other things. Sometimes she came home with shopping bags full of new clothes, or the closets would be rearranged. Or she woke me up early on Saturday mornings, when she knew I liked to sleep late, just to talk.

Nikita was always making plans, plans, plans. Seemed as if every week it was something else—if not some changes she wanted to start up at her office, it was a trip, or some promotional scheme to sell my books, or something.

Wore me down, day by day. All I wanted was a place that was a haven, away from all the madness of the street, the tension at the recording studio, the pressure of reporters hounding me for interviews. That's what home meant to me, a place where I could shut the world out, cleanse myself. Niki was just the opposite. She wanted, needed, to bring the world home with her every day, into our lives, into our heads. The only time the world didn't interfere was when we made love. Then nothing else mattered.

I guess after a while we found some sort of middle ground, a way to deal with each other. It was never really a compromise. It was just not talking about the things that bothered us, as if they would mysteriously go away if we didn't, and then we could keep the shaky peace we had. Sometimes it reminded me of rival gangs on either side of the desired turf, wary of crossing the line, both wanting the same thing but not knowing how to share it, ya know?

I'm not sure when the need hit—to have a family. I thought it would ground us, settle us somehow, but it was more than that. There was something deep inside me that felt it would make *me* whole, that it would be something, someone, who was mine, that I could care for, the way that Lacy and I had never been cared for as kids. I wanted to do that.

That's when the next battle between Nikita and I started. Every time I'd bring it up, she'd find a way to shoot it down. I started staying out more. She started complaining, so I stayed out more, which only gave her more fuel for her fire of reasons why we weren't ready to have kids.

The whole topic rose like a wall between us. We both knew what was on the other side, but no one wanted to be the first to cross over.

That morning after I walked out and drove around, I went to see Remy, an old buddy of mine—sort of a godfather to me, since I never knew who my father was. We talked about the old days, and joked about how I'd made something of myself. He said he was proud of me, proud of all I'd accomplished.

"I was really worried about you son, after Lacy. But you pulled yourself together, got yourself a good woman and made a life."

"You helped a lot. If you hadn't given me that first job, I don't know what I would've done."

He chuckled and clapped me on the back. "Son, as determined as you was to take care of you and yo' sister, you would've found a way. Just glad I was able to do somethin'." He puffed on his cigarette. "How's things with you and yo' wife?"

"Fine." I didn't need to tell him what was going on with Nikita and me. That was private.

"Good. Every man needs a good woman. Wasn't meant to live on this earth alone."

"Yeah."

My pager went off. I checked the number. Home. It was the third time she'd paged me since I'd left hours earlier.

" 'Scuse me a minute." I went to the pay phone in the back and called.

"Quinn, we need to talk. Not tomorrow, not in the middle of the night. Please."

"About what, Niki?"

"About us. What's happening to us, and what we're going to do about it. I can't live like this anymore. And I don't think you want to, either."

"I'll be home when I get there. When I wanted to talk, all you wanted to give me was more ying yang."

I heard her sharp inhale.

"Where are you, Quinn?"

"Why?"

"Because if you don't plan to come here, I'll come there."

"Do what you want. You always do, anyway. Later." I hung up, disgusted again. All I needed was to have my woman come hunting me down. I'd be damned if I would go running home like some trained seal.

I went back to the table and ordered another Jack on the rocks.

"Everything cool, son?" Remy asked.

"Yeah. Everything is fine." I took a long swallow. "So, how's everything going with the business?"

It must have been about one o'clock in the morning by the time I rolled out of there and headed home. At least I was mellow enough to listen to whatever it was she had on her mind this time. I figured she'd be up waiting, as usual.

She wasn't.

SEVEN

Can't Let Go

The house was stone cold silent. After I checked out the parlor floor I tiptoed upstairs, halfway mindful of not disturbing Mrs. Finch, who swore she could hear every creak and whistle.

I opened the bedroom door and stepped further into the room. It was dark, save for a milky stream of light from the full moon that hung right outside my window. I eased the door closed, not wanting to wake Nikita if I didn't have to.

My eyes began to adjust to the dark, making out shapes and locations of furniture in the room. Something wasn't right.

I walked closer toward the bed, searching in the twilight for the familiar outline of Nikita's body.

The bed was empty.

Something gripped me, like that feeling you get when you're at the top of the roller coaster, held there for a moment, just before it makes its hurtling descent, when terror grabs hold of you and you want to get off. Too late. You're on your way down.

I stared harder, tried to force her image to be there. Then I saw the red light of the answering machine blinkings its warning in the dark.

"Nikita." I knew there'd be no answer, but I called her name, anyway. Nikita never left messages unanswered on the machine—if she were home.

Flipping on the light only confirmed what I already knew, but that didn't stop me from looking around as if I expected her to walk out of the bathroom or up the stairs. I walked through the adjoining bathroom to the front guest room that we'd converted into an office space, and looked out the window. Sometimes Niki did wild things at night, like taking a stroll to the all night store, because she said it was so peaceful in the neighborhood and walking relaxed her. I looked out the window. That's when I noticed that her car wasn't there. She hadn't walked to wherever she'd gone.

Looking for me.

My heart started beating a little faster, and a wave of unease rocked through my gut. I went back downstairs. Maybe she'd left a note.

I searched in the kitchen, the dining and living rooms. Nothing. This wasn't like her. No matter how late I'd stayed out in the past, she'd never just up and walked out, jumped in her car in the middle of the night to come looking for me.

Naw, that wasn't like her at all, no matter what she'd said on the phone. She probably just got pissed off and went to Parris and Nick's house. Yeah, that was probably it. My stomach began to settle.

I checked my watch. 2:30. Too late to call over there. She was probably on her way home, anyway.

I prowled around in the kitchen for a while and finally

decided to fix a sandwich and wash it down with a bottle of beer. Then I went upstairs.

Standing in the doorway of our bedroom, I experienced the first inkling of what Nikita felt when she sat up waiting for me all kinds of hours, thinking all sorts of things. Damn. I'd never really looked at it from her perspective before, not really. It was an empty feeling threaded with apprehension, the kind of twisted sensation that runs the full menu of emotions—annoyance, anger, dread, acceptance—then back up and down the scale again. Was this what I did to her? Was this what she'd been trying to explain all along?

I sat down on the side of the bed. Whenever she got in, we'd have to talk, try to work through this mess we'd gotten ourselves into, try to break down some of these walls, and talk—like we used to, in the beginning.

Yeah. We'd talk.

I lay back and tucked my hands behind my head and smiled.

At the same moment, the phone rang.

I sat up and turned toward the phone, caught a glimpse of the clock—*3:00 A.M.*—stretched, and reached for the phone. Probably Niki calling to say she was on her way.

"Hello?"

"Mr. Parker?"

The blood started to pound in my ears. "Yeah. Who's this?"

"Mr. Parker, I'm calling from St. Luke's Hospital."

Something powerful gripped my chest, cutting off the air.

"Your wife, Nikita was in a very serious car accident, Mr. Parker. You need to get here right away. We've left several messages . . ."

Suddenly, the flashing red light on the machine seemed to glow like the neon lights on Broadway, blinding, overpowering.

"W—how is she? What happened?"

"The doctor will talk with you when you arrive. Please hurry."

I slammed down the phone, but for a few seconds I was paralyzed—with fear. I couldn't get my body to respond. Questions tumbled unchecked through my head, then propelled me forward toward the answers.

I ran down the stairs, grabbed my keys from that antique table in the hall, and sprinted out the door. Tearing away from the curb, I freed myself to concentrate, trying to think where the damn hospital was. Then it hit me. It was the same hospital where they'd first taken Lacy.

My stomach rolled, and heat rushed to my head. "No! Not again, *please.*"

When I ran through the swinging hospital doors everything suddenly seemed to crawl in slow motion. I felt as if I'd stepped outside of my body into a foreign world. Exhausted looking doctors and harried nurses wound in and out of each other like weatherbeaten threads of a rope—one sturdy unit—yet remaining separate and distinct with their charts, questions, commands, and clanging equipment. The howling, static–filled intercom blared out indiscernible announcements that bounced off pale green walls and stretchers laden with the ill and wounded.

I was invisible to all but myself. Everyone was engulfed in their own moment in time, oblivious to my need to know.

That need pushed me forward, one heavy step at a time, until I reached the front desk.

"I want to know where my wife is," I demanded of the woman behind the horseshoe–shaped counter.

She barely looked up at me, keeping her limited attention span focused on her phone conversation. She held up her hand, as if signaling to me that whatever reason I had come could wait. Then, as if she had second thoughts, she pushed a clipboard with a form attached and a blue Bic pen dangling from a springy rubber band toward me.

All the little check–off boxes of multiple choice ailments began dancing across the page. My eyes rolled up from the paper weight of diversion—that's all those forms are, you know, a means to keep you busy so that you won't freak, and keep your mind off why you are there—and rested on the woman's face behind the desk.

She slowly turned her gaze toward me, her eyes weary from everything they'd witnessed, remaining in place more as symbols than tools, her entire expression a blank page.

"You need to fill that out—"

I leaned dangerously close, close enough to know she'd eaten chili for dinner, so close her head snapped back in surprise. I pressed my palms against the desk to keep from snatching her from behind it. "My wife, Nikita Parker, was brought here. She was in a car accident. I want to know where she is. Now." Each word was spat with precision, even as my thoughts spun and my world seemed to be dissolving. I could see her flinch at each word that was shot at her like a poison dart, clean, targeted so that she no longer retained any doubts about why I was there, in her face, at 3:30 in the morning.

"I—I'm sorry. I thought—" She turned toward her computer screen and began to type. "She's still in emergency." My stomach roiled. "Trauma Room Six. Around that corner and to the left."

I spun away in the direction of her elongated finger, trying to keep the floor from slipping beneath my feet. She was saying something about not being sure if they'd let me in, but I acted as if I didn't hear her, because suddenly this wasn't a dream anymore. I couldn't just blink real hard, or turn over and wake up. The instant she found Nikita's name in the computer confirmed everything I'd been dreading since I got the call.

Bumping and weaving past people, I finally found Trauma Room Six. I could feel my chest heave and the knot in my belly grow tighter, squeezing. I stepped closer, just as a nurse came pushing out of the swinging doors, her green gown spattered with blood. *Niki's blood*. A wave of terror roared through me, taking my breath away.

The nurse started past me. I grabbed her arm. She turned, momentarily startled—annoyed.

"My wife. Nikita Parker."

Her eyes widened, and something akin to sorrow moved like a shadow across her pale pink face.

"We're trying to stabilize her now."

"How . . . bad?"

"I'm sorry. The doctor will have to talk with you as soon as he can."

"I have to see her."

"You can't. Not now. They're working on her."

"No. You don't understand. I *have* to."

She put her hand on my shoulder. "I do understand. But we're trying to save your wife's life, and you're being in there isn't going to help us to do that. Please. I know it's hard, but you've got to wait."

She hurried off, leaving me with visions I didn't want to see, words I didn't want to hear spreading like scattergun shots through my head.

I turned toward the door she'd exited and got jostled by an orderly jogging down the cluttered corridor. Perhaps it was my signal to go away, because when I turned back my gaze met the square glass panel of the door, which sucked me inside its vacuum–like interior, where it collected the debris of destruction.

Slithering, snake–like tubes sprouted from horror movie machines, ran along the floors between paper–covered shoes rising to the long metal table, disappearing beneath stained sheets to the motionless form beneath.

Then all at once there was a frantic flurry of activity, as if everyone had been jolted by a stream of unseen electricity. Machines beeped a long, high pitched warning, and doctors shouted out orders. One approached the form on the table.

"Clear!" The pads he held in his hands were pressed down on her bare chest.

Her body arched from the waist and fell back with a dull, thudding noise.

The doctor looked at the machine watching for the crest in the flat white line that crawled across the panel.

"Clear!"

Her tiny body rocked again, vibrating through mine. I felt my muscles stiffen, my heart seize.

Beep. Beep. Beep.

The doctor nodded. A nurse pulled the sheet up to her chin to cover her nakedness.

"Let's get her out of here," the savior instructed.

It took four of them to push the heavy–wheeled table with the small body on top of it. They burst through the swinging doors.

"Almost lost her," the savior said to his apostle.

They pushed past me. Invisible me. I pulled the savior away from the table, and that's when I saw her face. My insides lurched as I grabbed the side of the bed to keep from falling. *Not my Niki.*

"You've got to let us get her to OR, sir."

It was the savior.

"I'm her husband. I've got to talk to her. Please."

"Quinn." The word was barely a whisper, as if only conjured from my imagination.

I grabbed her hand, pressing my face close to hers as we all trotted down the corridor.

"I'm here, Baby. I'm here."

"I—sorry—wasn't—payin'—attention."

"I'm sorry, too. For everything. For making it hard on you. But it's all right. You're going to be all right. You have to be. For me. For us."

"Didn't mean what—I said—this morning. Scared—
I'd—make a—lousy mom—like mine."

"We can have all the babies we want. When you're better.
When we're ready. Just like you said."

"Promise—you won't stop—reaching—for everything
—I've always seen—in you. The best. Or all of—what we've
been—was for nothing. You have to see."

"You *are* my vision." I squeezed her hand. "*I* was nothing
before you came into my life." I pushed a blood–crusted
lock of hair away from her face. "Livin' day–to–day on
the edge, with no direction, no goals. You brought order
to my world, put it at my feet, told me I could take it, make
it mine. For all the strength I was supposed to possess,
you're my real strength, what makes me get up every day
and try again."

My throat seemed to close, but I had to force the words
out. She must hear me, must know.

"I need you, Nikita. I've never needed anybody in my
life, but I do need you. Should have told you how much.
Every day. The difference you make in my life. We're just
getting the hang of this lovin' thing. We have the rest of
our lives to get it right. You and me, Baby. Whatever it
takes. For you. Anything."

"No. *For you.* For once—for you. True to yourself, whatever it means. Love yourself like—I've always loved you."

"It's my fault, Baby. I should have come home."

"Choices," she choked out. "We . . . all make choices."

It looked as if she tried to smile, but it was more like
her mouth twisted in pain, and then her eyes rolled back
in her head. She squeezed my hand hard and let out a
whimper. "Love you, Q." A tear slid down her battered
face. "Don't want to die."

"Oh, God. I love you. Don't you leave me, Niki. We got
things to do, Baby."

"Do it—for you. Always there—inside you."

"We must get her into OR, Mr. Parker—now," the savior said. "You'll have to wait."

They rolled her away, through the swinging metal doors, away from me, from the strength I needed to pour into her—to keep her with me.

I don't know how long I stood there, minutes, hours, staring at the door imagining that any minute Niki would come strutting out with that walk of hers. Man, she had a walk that blew my mind from the first day I saw her—slow and sensual, but not provocative. Just right, ya know? But everything about her was just right. Not too much or too little of anything. And that smile. Man, when she smiled at me, it felt like my whole world lit up like the Fourth of July.

How could the light go out of my world? She was always so careful when she drove, always telling me to slow down and watch out for the other guy.

At first it used to get on my nerves, as if she thought I didn't have good sense, didn't realize that I'd been driving since I was fifteen, when I hot–wired that banged up Chevy. *Humph.* Never told her about that. She would've had a fit. She was like that, always worried about one thing or the other, even if it was years after the fact.

"You're a name now, Quinn," she'd said one day when we were just hanging out at Bryant Park enjoying a live concert. Think it was Sonny Rollins. Yeah, yeah it was. She said, "Pretty soon, Baby, you're going to be really large. You don't want all kinds of stuff to come back and haunt you. You know how they like to dig up stuff on folks once they're out there."

"I'm not that important, Babe."

"That's what you think. You don't take your success seriously enough." She cuddled up closer, and I wrapped my arms around her.

"It's not about success, Niki. It's about how I live my life for me and you. Yeah, things are easier. We're not strugglin'. And yeah, sometimes folks recognize me on the street. No doubt. But hey, I'm still me.''

"I know, Baby, but I have such dreams for you, Quinn. You're so incredibly talented. I want the world to stand up and take notice, and I'm going to sit back grinning. 'That's my man.' "

I kissed the top of her head and laughed, feeling full and loved. Niki had a way with her, a way that made me feel like the king of the world, able to leap tall buildings without even getting out of bed. And I loved her for it.

I didn't say it much. I know that. But I tried to show her by doing things. Like, when I was cruising around the city and I saw something that I knew she'd really dig, or something that would make her laugh—Man, that laugh, like bells—I'd get it for her.

I remember one time I was uptown at one of those novelty shops and I saw a square plastic box that looked like a moving crate. It had all kinds of tags and stamps on it, and when you touched it there was a knocking sound and a little squeaky voice coming from inside saying, 'Hey! Hey you, let me out. Let me out of here!'' Then the box started vibrating. Knew I had to have it for her.

Got it gift wrapped, and when she opened the package and that box started doing its thing, she fell out laughing. Laughed so hard there were tears rolling down her cheeks. She played with that thing all night, just like a little kid.

See, stuff like that made me happy—just seeing her smile. She knew I had the loot to buy her just about anything she wanted, and she had her own, too. No doubt. But it was the little things she liked most.

Like sometimes in the dead of night, she'd tiptoe downstairs and keep me company when I was struggling over a new song, or trying to work out a scene in a book. She didn't say much, just sat curled up in a little ball on the couch, letting me know she was there if I needed her. Sometimes just her being there was all I needed, and suddenly everything would come together. The notes would fall in place, or the scene would unfold like a movie. She'd smile and say, "I knew you could do it. Don't ever stop believing that."

It was as if no matter what I did, what I was up against, what doubts I had, she never wavered in her faith in me, her trust that I would find what I needed to get the job done—inside me. *Hmm.* She was something.

She couldn't cook, though. Man, if I'd married her because I thought she could cook, I would've been in serious trouble. Girl couldn't boil water. But she tried. Sometimes on Saturday afternoons when I wasn't rehearsing, we'd spend some time in the kitchen. I'd try to show her a few things. And she'd look at me all wide-eyed and innocent, and mess it up every time. It was a standing joke between us. That, and too many other things. Too many other things.

So, I was just standing there, staring at the swinging door—the smell of disinfectant stinging my nose, the sounds seeping into my soul—thinking all this stuff, seeing everything that happened to us from the time we met, hopeful, ya know? I even prayed a minute. Can't remember the last time I prayed. I know I was stumbling over the words 'cause I didn't know what to say, how to say it. Just kept asking for her not to be taken from me. Give me a chance to do right. Give us a chance to make a life together.

Then the doors swung open, and I could feel myself breathing heavily, as if I'd been running. And the savior was walking toward me, pulling his cloth hat off his head. He wouldn't meet my eyes. And I knew, I just knew, but I needed to hear him tell me, to make him tell me that my world had come to an end.

He stepped up to me, looked in my eyes. "I'm sorry, Mr. Parker. We did everything in our power, used all our capabilities. But your wife's injuries were too severe. I'm sorry."

He hung his head and walked away. . . .

I turned away from the window, then, from our garden.
My bedroom came back into focus. "Who's there to laugh
and joke with me now, Mrs. Finch, make me whole? 'Cause
I feel like I'm unravelin', comin' apart piece by piece.
Nothin' matters. Nothin.' I just keep wantin' to go back
and fill in all the gaps, remind her how important she was
to me."

"She always knew, Quinten. What she saw in you, what
she wanted for you, can't be taken away because she's no
longer here to remind you. It's inside you. Just like Nikita
said. But you have to want it for yourself, not for anyone
else."

She got up from the edge of the bed and walked toward
me, gathered me in her arms and rocked me like a baby.
The shudders vibrated through me, but she held on to me
anyway, and I didn't care.

"It will be all right, son," she whispered, patting my
back. "It will. She left you with precious gifts, Quinten—
your memories, an ability to love, and a sense of yourself
that you never had before. Trust what she saw in you. Don't
betray that trust."

Slowly she released me, then stroked my cheek. "Get
some rest. Tomorrow will soon come." She turned and
walked out, closing my bedroom door softly behind her.

Tomorrow.

EIGHT

If Only You Knew

I stayed up most of the night, prowling around the house, remembering things I thought I'd forgotten. Funny, but even though I knew in my head that Nikita was gone, in my heart and soul she was still with me. It was a strange sensation, ya know? She was there in the scent of her that still lingered in our bedroom, in the special touches in our home, in her brush that still held strands of her hair threaded through it, the stacks of notes that she'd prepared on the manuscripts she was buying.

If I closed my eyes and listened to the quiet sounds of the house, I could almost hear her call my name.

All these thoughts and feelings rolled around in my head until the only way I felt I could free myself from the chains of sorrow was to break them down into words. So I wrote— from the bottom of my soul, pouring out things I'd kept buried in my heart, only half saying them when it was almost too late.

In them I found a small slice of comfort, even if it was only for the moment, as I tried to recapture the woman who had changed my life.

But morning came too soon. The sun shot bands of orange and gold through the bedroom window, burning my eyes, which had gotten used to the twilight of the room.

I looked down at the pages I'd written, surprised at what I saw, the emotion and images I'd captured. All I could hope was that everyone who listened would see Nikita as I did.

Running my hand across the pale white sheets of paper, I was like a blind person trying to read raised letters. I wanted to absorb the words, transform them into her, make her real, not just a memory. Word made flesh.

But the sounds of another day—car horns honking, the metal ring of garbage cans being hauled out to the curb, the high wails of a catfight in the backyard—slowly pushed their way into my world, reminding me that life goes on.

I looked around, knowing I couldn't stop the march of time, not with words, not with wishes, not with booze or endless hours of sleep. There was nothing I could do except hope that the awesomeness of living didn't swallow me whole.

Moving across the room a half step at a time, I got ready to face my day. Nick was coming to the house at seven, he'd said.

Don't know what I would've done without Nick Hunter. He'd always proven what a decent brother he was. It started long before Niki died when I'd walked into his club, *Rhythms,* and he'd heard me play that baby grand, and offered me a gig with his band on the spot.

Man, every time I thought about it I realized how lucky I was. Matter-of-fact, if I hadn't been hanging around playing I never would've officially met Nikita. We'd bumped into each other once before, when I was moving into my crib in the Village. Never thought I'd see her again. Then bam. She walked into the club that day, and then come to find out her best friend, Parris, was married to the brother.

Small world. No doubt.

I walked to the front of the house and peeked out from behind the curtains. Parked across the street was a news van, and several reporter types were hanging around drinking coffee.

Pushing the curtains back to block out the sight of the vultures, I turned away. I'd had to unplug the phone to stop the calls from reporters, not to mention Nikita's parents, who had no problem dropping their anguish into my lap, accusing me of being the cause of it all. If I hadn't been in her life, taken her out of her world, she'd still be alive. They didn't care that I'd lost her, too. I killed her. Stole her life.

I hadn't been out of the house since I'd come back from the hospital, to avoid being pounced upon by those who wanted to know "how I felt."

How the hell did they think I felt? Was this what Nikita had meant by success—your every move chronicled for the world to see—your pain and your joy, your failure? The height that she wanted to reach, where your life became fair game, to view and dissect? This burden of putting on a face for the world because it was expected? Why would anyone want that—to achieve so much that the world sat on the edge of its collective seats waiting for "success" to be taken away, so that they could flaunt it on their shows and in their newspapers. It was never anything I'd wanted. I didn't need to be recognized on the street or asked my life history from every reporter with a byline.

I'd always been a private person, keeping my thoughts and feelings close to the chest. It was the way I'd always been, trained like that from the street. There was no room for true confessions, opening yourself up. To do that could bring you down.

With Niki I'd tried to be different, open, but it was still hard. I guess that's why it had always been easier to express myself in written words and in music. Those things didn't leave me open, vulnerable.

I looked at the two page poem I'd written for Nikita. Maybe, if she was watching, listening, she'd hear the words I'd never said.

The knock at my bedroom door pulled me away, toward the inevitable.

" 'Mornin', Mrs. Finch." I stepped away, leaving the door open. Knew she was going to come in, anyway.

"How you feelin' this mornin', son?" She closed the door.

" 'Bout the same." I tried to smile.

She patted my shoulder. "The car just pulled up out front."

My stomach dipped. I nodded my head, not willing to trust my voice.

"Nick should be here soon."

I nodded again.

"You want me to fix you something to eat?"

"Not hungry."

"You should try, Quinten. Gonna be a long day."

"Hmmm."

"I'll bring something and leave it in the kitchen. Just in case," she added, walking toward to the door.

When it closed, I opened the closet and took out my suit. As much as I hated wearing one, I knew it was expected.

I looked at it for a minute—navy blue, single-breasted, Armani, fit like it was made just for me, and it was. Nikita made sure of that. She'd bought it for me on my last birthday.

Ironic, *huh?*

By the time I was halfway dressed I heard the doorbell. *Probably Nick.* I buttoned my shirt and went downstairs to let him in.

"Hey, Man." Nick slid his dark glasses off his nose and hugged me, patting my back. Together as always, Nick with his cool brown skin and sprinkles of salt in his dark hair. He looked exactly as he did on his many CD covers— confident, and in control.

"Hey," I mumbled, catching a glimpse of his wife, Parris, standing behind him. I stepped to the side, letting them pass.

When I'd first met Parris, I thought next to Nikita, she was one of the most beautiful women I'd ever met. She had jet black hair that she always wore loose framing her olive-toned face. But it was her eyes that caught and held you—green, the color of money. Looking at them now, a united front, I envied what they had. I know it couldn't be easy on their marriage with Nick constantly on tour with the band, or in the studio. Not to mention that Parris had made it as a singer so successfully in Europe that she was out of the country several months a year. But, man, when they were together you could see their love snap back and forth between them. There was no competition, no tension, no trying to prove anything to each other. They were like a perfect symphony, blending together.

I'd wanted that with Niki, a sense of balance and harmony. As much as we loved each other, there was never a feeling of real peace between us. Just beneath the surface, there were always rumblings, like a volcano poised to erupt.

"How are you, Babe?" Parris asked, kissing my cheek.

"Cool. Come on in." I closed the door behind her, took a breath that I hoped would calm my unruly belly—then followed them into the living room.

Nick and Parris sat on the couch, looking at me as if they expected me to fall on my face. I started to pace, the observation making me even more unsteady, not sure how I was supposed to act, what I was supposed to say. I was a zombie. All I knew was that I felt like I was outside myself in some unreal world, and all this was happening to somebody else. But it wasn't. I dreaded what the day would bring.

"Can I do anything, Quinn?" Parris asked.

"Naw. Can't think of anything." I wanted to fix myself a drink, take the edge off, but I knew that wouldn't help. " 'Scuse me a minute."

I went in the kitchen, pressed my head against the cool metal of the refrigerator door, and closed my eyes. I could feel the waves of pain trying to take over, swell and pull me under.

I felt a hand on my shoulder. Slowly, I raised my head and turned to face my friend.

"You feel like talking, Man?" Nick asked, his eyes searching my gloom for signs of life.

"Nick, Man, I wouldn't even know what to say."

"I know it's going to be hard. But I'm here."

"Yeah."

"Maybe after everything is settled you should think about getting away for a while."

"Yeah, maybe. I don't know. Right now, I—I can't think straight. It takes all my energy to just get through the day." I sat down at the kitchen table. Nick took a seat opposite me.

"Been getting any rest?"

"Naw. Not really."

"You know we have to get back into the studio pretty soon."

"Yeah. You probably should think about getting somebody else to complete the CD."

"Listen, maybe this isn't the time to say this. I don't know. But even as hard as this is, you can't let your life come to a halt. Part of who you are is your music. Your ability to convey emotion through your playing. Through your writing."

"The desire is gone, Nick. It's like the fire that's always

been lit in my gut has been put out. Can you understand that?"

He looked down at his hands for a minute—I guess trying to figure out how to cross the bridge and reach me—but the path that led to me was full of broken, rotted planks of scarred, cracked wood, ready to give way at the slightest bit of pressure. Nick couldn't reach me. Nobody could, not without risk to themselves. And I no longer had the will to steer them along the course to safety. I was locked away inside myself.

"Just give yourself some time, Q. Give in to how you feel. Just don't give up, Brother.

"I think I heard the car horn," Nick said, then stood. "We probably need to get ready to head to the church."

I'd thought I'd heard it too, while we were sitting there listening to the rift that hung between us, but I'd wanted to ignore it.

"In a minute."

He nodded and walked back up front. I followed shortly after, determined that I would get through this day. And when I did, maybe I could start thinking about how to get through the next one.

The instant we set foot outside, the reporters, photographers, and cameramen from *Eyewitness News* circled us, like rampaging Indians around a wagon train.

Nick held my arm on one side, Mrs. Finch the other, and tried to usher me through the crowd. But once they recognized him and then Parris—whose face appeared on so many magazine covers and music videos across the country—they became fair game, too.

Suddenly I stopped. I knew I couldn't get through, and deal with, what was ahead if I didn't handle this now.

I held up my hand. "This will be my one and only statement, and then I'd appreciate it if you all gave us some privacy. We're all, everyone who knew and loved my wife, going through a very difficult time dealing with her loss. Nikita was a very public person. I never have been. I know this isn't what she would have wanted. She'd want you to write about the vitality of life, what she represented. Not this. Not trying to chronicle our pain and sorrow. It's not how she would have wanted to be remembered. Thank you for understanding."

The Red Sea of voyeurs parted, suddenly silenced, flash-bulbs stilled. Maybe in respect. I didn't know. It didn't matter. I just wanted it to be over.

The limousine driver opened the door and we filed in. He slammed it behind us, and that sinking sensation grabbed hold again, trying to pull me under. But I saw Niki's smile, heard Mrs. Finch's and Niki's words, and I knew I had to find a way to stay afloat.

By the time we pulled up at the church, the cars were double parked almost for the entire length of the block, on both sides.

As soon as I stepped out, I saw Nikita's folks walking into the church. Her mother, maybe sensing my presence, turned toward me. For an instant our gazes met. Her eyes pinched at the corners and I could see her nostrils flare even from where I stood. I wasn't sure if it was pain or hatred simmering there. Whatever it was, it was directed at me.

Again flashbulbs popped, as we walked the gauntlet to the church entrance, but at a discreet distance.

Patting the breast pocket of my jacket, I felt and heard the crackle of the white paper and drew strength from the words.

As I lowered my head and walked down the church aisle an all too familiar hand gently clasped my arm.

I knew even before I saw her that it was Maxine. My gaze ran from the long, slender fingers along the chocolate brown arm until it rested on her face. She offered me a tight smile and the warmth of her eyes. Just her being there meant more to me than she could imagine. She still

looked as great as I remembered—sleek—maybe better.
San Francisco had treated her well.

"Thanks for coming," I whispered, squeezing her hand
for a moment.

She nodded and I moved on.

I found my way to the front of the church and sat,
listening, as one after another, friends, family, stood and
remembered Nikita Harrell Parker. The words of the minis-
ter rose and fell in powerful crests of testament that I
couldn't hear. What did he really know about her? Only
what he'd been told by her parents, who knew little or
nothing about their daughter. What did any of them know?

All too soon I faced them, suddenly not caring if they
understood her, just that they listened to the words I desperately needed to say. To her.

Staring out across the patchwork quilt of faces, I recognized many—some from the publishing world and some
from the music industry, many who were neither.

What suddenly struck me hardest was realizing they were
there as friends, supporters, people who truly cared about
her even if they hadn't really understood her. Maybe they
were looking for a way to ease the hurt, too.

Slowly I pulled the two pieces of white paper from my
pocket, spread them on the lectern.

Mrs. Finch, Sean and *Khendra, Ms. Ingram,*—Niki's former
boss—*Remy* and *T.C.*—from the neighborhood—*Jewel* and
Taj,—old friends of Niki's—*Nick* and *Parris, Val* and *Maxine, Amy, Grant*—Niki's ex—and *Nikita's family*. They were
all there.

I hoped they would all understand. I took a deep breath
and let the words flow.

> Too short the time we had
> To make the most of it
> Too soon our dreams realized
> Not long enough to savor

The souls of who we were to
Each other, we fought together
And against the odds
Me and you, Baby
Mine, always in my soul
Giving, living
Loving you in all I can do
Not always in the words I speak
For that I will always wish
For more time to say
I love you, my life
My wife, my meaning
For opening my eyes
And saying I can
Even when I couldn't
Knowing that you wouldn't
Let me ever believe less,
Now without you
I wander aimless, adrift
Struggling to find the safety
Of your arms, your smile
That lights my way
Your vibrancy that electrified
The melody of my soul I gave only to you
My love, I know I must find my own way, Now
Without you it will be impossible
But I will, for you as always
And now me
Forever I will love you
I will.

With care I folded the pages and returned them to my pocket, next to my heart.

I stepped down, and everything in front of me began blending together in a medley of brilliant color and light. I wouldn't cry. I couldn't break. Not now. Because if I did, my own river of sorrow would never end—not ever. When I ran my hand across the cool, mahogany surface that held her on a bed of soft velvet, I knew that what lay ahead of me was a future without her, and I must find the strength she saw in me to move on, however long it took.

MAXINE

NINE

Revelations

The shock of seeing Quinn again was more difficult than I'd imagined. I thought I was prepared. I wasn't.

Most of the night before, Val and I stayed up talking, catching up, sharing. Mostly we talked about Quinn. Me. Taylor. And Jamel. This complex collection of souls.

"There's no easy way, Maxine. I'm sure I'm not telling you something you don't already know. But if you don't do this now, who knows how many years it will be before you will?" Val tucked her legs beneath her and leaned back against the cushions of the couch.

I sipped my margarita.

"What's happening with you and Taylor? How's he handling this?"

I swallowed and looked out toward the backyard from her living room window. "He left me. I think."

Valarie frowned and craned her neck toward me. "What? What do you mean, you *think* he left you?"

"He told me he thought it was good that I was coming to New York to settle this thing with me and Quinn, but he wouldn't be there when I got back."

"Oh, Max. I'm so sorry. I—I probably shouldn't have even asked you to come. This—"

"We make choices, Val. This has nothing to do with you. I chose to come. I chose to handle my life the way I have. Now I have to deal with it."

"What are you going to do if Taylor doesn't come back, Maxine? And, God, what about Jamel?"

I took another sip of my drink. "I have to find a way, find the words to convince this man that I love him, how much he means to me and to Jamel. And that nothing and no one else matters. I'm not sure how to make all this up to him, but I know I've got to try. I have to tell him the things I didn't get to say."

I took a breath. "Val, on my way out here I had some time to really think about things. Things between Taylor and me. Who we are. And I realized that as much as I felt for Quinten Parker, it could no longer compare to what I feel for Taylor. Taylor opened his soul to me, Val, with all my baggage, closed the doors behind me, and never let the past creep in."

Val shook her head. "That sounds a lot like gratitude, Maxine. Not love."

"Gratitude! How could you think that? I didn't have to stay with Taylor. I'm there because I want to be. He makes me happy, and I think I make him happy. We've built a life and a family together that I wouldn't trade for anything." I got up and crossed the room to the small bar and refreshed my drink. Two was my limit.

"Taylor could have walked away a long time ago. He didn't. Which shows the kind of man he is. What Taylor and I have, I never had with Quinn. Quinn and I were always on the verge of collapse. I lived in a quiet state of anxiety, wondering when the fairy tale of our relationship was going to end.

"Sure, there was plenty of passion and lust. There was a depth of friendship, and a sense of the familiar. Even a level of love. But not the kind you build a life on. I know that now. It's not like that with me and Taylor. What we have is solid." I sat back down and looked across at Val, who was smiling as if she held the secret to immortality.

"What?"

"I'm glad you finally got it out, Maxie. After all these years and all this time. You needed to say the words—that what you and Quinn shared was special, yes, unequaled, yes, but at the heart of it was a childhood fantasy come true. That basis of what was needed to make it real was never really there. Honestly. It was two *friends* who found their way to each other in a time of need. And as long as you keep those words, those thoughts, with you, and believe them in your heart, you'll find the right words to tell Quinn about Jamel and the strength to go home and seal your relationship with Taylor once and for all.

"How do you think Q is going to handle the fact that he has a three–year–old son he knew nothing about?" Her eyes bore into mine, and I suddenly realized how effective she would be in the courtroom. My stomach dipped.

"I don't know," I answered truthfully. "In my head I've seen all the scenarios, Val. From titanic fury to "Baby, I love you, let's get married," and everything in between. I have to find that familiar place that was always between us, find a way to get us there, so that he will understand that what I did was never out of hurt, revenge, or selfishness. I did it for him."

Val looked into my eyes. Her voice lowered, and she took my hand. "Be absolutely sure, Maxine. Really. Because if there is one grain of uncertainty, one kernel of untruth, Quinn will see it, and he'll never forgive you. And neither will Taylor."

I thought about our conversation as we filed out of the church, and Q's words to Nikita echoed in my head. He loved her the way I loved Taylor, a way Q and I could never love each other. And finally it was okay.

We stepped out into the blazing morning sunshine. It had been a long time since my sunshine wasn't filtered by smog. For a moment I smiled, forgetting where I was and why, and I turned my face toward the sun, letting its beams bathe me in its warm strength.

When I looked around there were throngs of people headed toward their cars. Reporters and cameramen were recording the unfolding of events, and my heart ached for Quinn. I knew what a private person he was, how he never wanted to be in the spotlight. I couldn't begin to imagine what this, compounded with his loss of Nikita, must be doing to him.

Instinct wanted me to run to him, put my arms around him, and make the hurt go away. But I no longer had the illusions of naïveté.

Someone grabbed me from behind and turned me around.

My eyes widened. "Remy!"

"Hey, Girl."

He squeezed me to him, and I caught the faint clinging smell of cigars, cigarettes, and years of Harlem hustle. It made me smile.

I squeezed him back, giving him a quick once over. "Still looking good, Remy."

"Got to. Got to. You ain't lookin' too bad, yo'self. Life on the coast seem like it's treatin' you real good."

"Yes. It is." I smiled.

He patted my shoulder. " 'Sho glad you could come, Max. Q need all the friends he kin get. Tough time for him. Tough time."

"I'm glad I'm here, too, Remy."

"Hey, Val." He kissed her cheek. "How's the lawyering business?"

"Just fine, Remy."

"You ladies need a ride? I'd be happy to take you."

"Val has her car, but thanks, anyway."

"How long you in town?"

"I'm leaving today."

"Too bad. Thought you might have a chance to talk. Maybe next time."

"Yes. Maybe."

"You take care now, Max. It was damned good to see you, Girl."

I smiled. "You too, Remy."

"Bye, Val. Ever need an attorney, I'm gon' look you up. Proud of you, Girl."

"You do that, Remy. And thanks."

We watched him walk off, and he quickly got lost in the crowd ahead of us, who for the most part towered over his mere five–foot–five height.

Val turned to me, and asked if I was ready.

I took a breath and nodded. We headed for her car and followed the solemn procession away from the church, both silently hoping that the next phase would be quick and as painless as possible for Quinn. And for the most part it was, or so I thought. He held himself in stoic silence while the reverend said the final words.

"When are you going to talk to him?" Val asked as we watched the last of the mourners return to their cars and drive away from the cemetery.

"Now just seems so inappropriate, you know? Between all this, the reporters dogging his trail, and Nikita's parents snubbing him as if he has the plague—" I shook my head. "How much can one person take in a day?"

"If you look for excuses, you'll be sure to find them, Maxine. No time is good, but there's none like the present."

She raised her chin and I followed its angle until I saw Quinn standing alone in the distance.

"I'll wait for you in the car. However long it takes." She started walking across the rolling hills of grass. My heart hammered.

"Val, wait."

She kept going, even as hard as I prayed for her to turn back around, grab my arm and take me back to the car. But the time for running, not confronting and dealing with the things that were hard and painful was past.

I turned back toward where I'd seen Quinn. He was leaning against a tree, smoking a cigarette, a long dark figure conjuring up an image of a carved African warrior highly polished but dulled by time and circumstance, but still magnificent—sent out by the chieftan to stand watch. I suddenly wondered when he'd started smoking. It was an odd thing to think at the time, but it just came to me. I guess my nerves were making my thoughts go wild, trying to confuse the issue.

There were probably too many things I didn't know about Quinten Parker, although there was a time when I thought I knew him well. I thought I could see into his soul and touch it somehow, make it—him—a part of me. Perhaps in a way I did—with Jamel. Quinn left that part of himself with me—the little boy he'd rarely had the chance to be.

My heart beat a bit faster, and a gentle wave of sadness flowed through my veins. We were two different people now, living separate lives, with separate goals.

I supposed I could have stood there forever watching him, this man I had once loved, watched him in all his aching beauty and wondered if things could have been different between us. If I'd called him, even though it *was* a week before his wedding, would he have called it off and come to me? Would he have grown to resent me for "trapping" him, taking him away from Nikita? Would he have been the man I needed to be the father of my child—this the most important of duties—when he was still struggling to be a man? It was that doubt that made me hesitate, then. That doubt and the fear that I could be responsible for snatching away the happiness he'd finally found. And because of that doubt, that fear, I couldn't confront him. Why now? I'd walked away from telling him, taking on all the roles myself because of my misgivings. I couldn't walk away again. I was certain of what I must do. Even though Quinn may not have been the father I needed—unable to fit that role—he still must have a place in his son's life. Would I be able to find the words?

I'd asked myself those questions and countless other variations of them over the years, and still did, even as I stood less than a hundred feet away from him. I didn't have the answers then, and only some of them now. All I could do was what I thought was best for everyone, and I could only hope and pray that he'd understand that.

I took a long, deep breath, inhaling the scents of freshly turned earth and cut green grass, hoping to fortify myself with a dose of nature at its purest, cleansing my thoughts, my heart, and my spirit so that I could face him openly and honestly.

I put one foot forward, and I wasn't sure if it was his instinctive street sense or the almost imperceptible sound of my footsteps on the moist grass that caused him to turn in my direction.

Even from that distance I could see the dark pools of pain swimming in his eyes, almost as if for those moments he'd been in another place, someplace that only he could reach. In the instant when he recognized me, a flicker of light danced in the darkness of his gaze and then dimmed. He turned his head and leaned back against the tree.

My intuition told me to run, fast and as far away from the fire that stood before me. Even though Quinn's blaze was momentarily snuffed, the embers that could easily burn me were still present, ready to be ignited.

"Hi, Q."

I saw his nostrils flair as if he struggled for air. I eased closer, close enough to feel the heat rise from his body. A shudder rippled along my spine.

He glanced briefly at me, his mouth flickering with the remnants of that smile of his. Then he looked back to that place where he'd been. "Good to see you, Max. Look great."

"It's good to see you, too, Q. I wish it didn't have to be like this. I'm really sorry about Nikita." I swallowed. "I know you loved her a great deal." I touched his arm, and I could feel the muscles knot beneath my fingertips.

His eyes cut in my direction, narrowing. "Yeah. You would know." I flinched. He looked down at my hand, then took it in his and gently squeezed it. "Funny how things work out, huh, Max?"

"Like what?" My heart was racing.

He ran his thumb thoughtfully along the outside of my hand as he held it. My entire body trembled.

"Me. You. Nikita."

I heard the hitch in his voice when he said her name.

"It was a beautiful poem you read in church. It said a lot," I offered, scrambling for something to help me gain my balance again.

"You can never say enough—sometimes. Ya know?"

I nodded. "Sometimes we hold on to the things in our hearts, thinking that there'll be time to say them." Images of all the times gone by came to me, when I never told him what was in my heart, what I wanted for us. I guess I just thought he'd know, or that there was always tomorrow.

He kept rubbing his thumb across my hand.

"That's what hurt me so much with Lacy, ya know?"

He turned his head away. I couldn't see his eyes, but I could see his Adam's apple working up and down. He was fighting to keep from crying, and that very notion took hold of me and wrang my insides. I'd only seen him break down that one time, the day he got the letter awarding him the money in Lacy's wrongful death suit. I saw him as always invincible, a tower of strength, even though I knew his feelings ran deep. He just wasn't someone to show them.

"I never got to tell her how I felt, how important she was in my life, and I've regretted it every day since—she was killed. I didn't want that to happen between me and Niki, ya know?" Slowly he shook his head, then lowered it. "But it was hard, Max. You know how it is on the street. Life is tough, fast, full of secrets, things you need to keep close to you so your words, feelings, weaknesses, can't be used against you."

He angled his chin and looked out across the sea of green grass with its rising gray tides of concrete and marble.

"Secrets are just like lies," he said, almost to himself.

My heart beat even faster. *Did he know?* "W—hat do you mean?"

"Nikita used to say that. "Secrets are just like lies.""

"May—be not—a lie. Maybe just a truth that's unspoken." I swallowed. "Not a lie."

"But once you start them they build and grow until you work so hard to keep them that you'll even lie to make sure your secret is safe. Secrets can hurt, Max. Even I learned that."

"Some secrets are meant to keep from hurting, from doing harm."

He looked at me then, as if he were trying to read the meaning behind my words. The right corner of his mouth curved just a bit. He blew out a long breath.

"You know one thing about you and I that I was always grateful for, Max?"

"What?"

"We were always up front, truthful with each other. Even when it hurt, ya know?" Slowly he nodded. "That's what it's about—at the root of it."

Oh, God, how was I going to do this? I heard the words rush around in my head. I needed to say them. He must hear them. My heart raced. My breathing escalated in rapid bursts as the words, *We have a son* rushed up from my belly, then hung suspended like clothes on a line, flapping recklessly, unable to get free. *Get it out and over, be branded a liar, a keeper of secrets.* But the words clung like lint in my throat. How could I hurt him, too?

"You think that's why the police tried to cover up what happened to Lacy? They didn't want to *hurt* or do *harm* to themselves with the truth? Probably why Nikita never told me you were leavin', either, huh?"

He glanced at me, another kind of sorrow in his eyes. The sorrow of time lost.

I didn't answer. I couldn't.

"Yeah, she finally told me. After we were married. I guess she was afraid, too."

"Of what?"

"You."

He reached into the inside pocket of his blue suit jacket, pulled out a box of Newports, lit one, and blew a thin cloud of smoke into the air. Birds nearby suddenly scattered, chirping and squawking as if the smoke were directed at them.

"Why?" I dared to ask. I needed to know, needed to hear him say it.

He looked at me through the white cloud, his lids partly lowered.

"She was afraid of our relationship. Everything you and I ever meant to each other. Our—friendship. The tie we had through Lacy, something she could never have."

But she had something I never had, your whole heart, I thought.

"So, she kept a secret to keep from hurting herself. Her unspoken truth. Until hidin' it became a lie." Slowly he nodded his head in acceptance and blew out smoke from between his teeth.

"We all get afraid sometimes, Q."

"No doubt. What do you do when you get scared, Max? Huh? I really need you to tell me, ya know? 'Cause that's how I'm feelin', Max, scared. Like everything is fallin' to pieces."

His gaze pierced me, entered my soul, begged me for an answer I couldn't give. To give it would force us to lose the one thing that still linked us to who we were with each other. *Trust.*

"I talk to a friend. Try to be honest with my feelings. Get it out of my system."

"Like we're doing now—talking like friends—being honest?"

I pressed my lips together and nodded.

My gaze followed the last gust of white smoke into the air, then watched the butt being crushed into the moist earth with the tip of his shoe, perfect, smooth as a well–choreographed dancestep. There was nothing rehearsed about Quinn. Never.

"Why did you really come, Maxie?"

The question, hurtled like a speeding ball, took my breath, widened my eyes.

He gave me that half smile. "You can tell me. Truth, remember—between friends? I know you didn't have any great love for Nikita."

His eyes held mine for a moment, and in that instant I felt that what he wanted was not really the truth, but to hear that I came because I *did* care about Nikita, that I'd forgiven him for breaking my heart, mangling my soul. Or maybe that's what I wanted to believe, to make the truth I held easier to let go. But there was still time, time to save us from more pain. I could lie. I could walk away from this place, let him believe what he wanted about my visit. But in my soul, in my heart, I knew I couldn't. Not again.

"Quinn. I—" I folded my arms. "I came because I am your friend. I care about you." I took a breath, hoping that the words would come gentle as the breeze that blew around us, not painful like the ache that had taken hold of my insides.

"I know, Max." He reached out and stroked my cheek. "I could always depend on you. You've always been there for me." He stepped closer and gathered me against him. His arms tightened around me, and he pressed his face against my hair.

"Thank you for comin', Max," he said in a hoarse whisper.

I felt a shudder run through him, and heard what sounded like a smothered sob catch in his throat. I slipped my arms around his waist. It felt so right, so good, even in this place, on this day. We held each other as we had when we found out his mother had abandoned him and when we buried Lacy, when we got the letter from the police department just before we made love for the very first time. The way we held each other when he came back home to tell me he was going to be with Nikita.

It was like all those times rolled into this one moment. I know he felt it, too.

"How long can you stay?"

"I'm going back tonight."

"Do you have to? Can't you stay a while longer? We could talk. I—"

The time for us was past. I accepted that. And with that acceptance was a sense of relief, completeness. I would always love Quinten Parker, but not the kind of love a life is built on. I had that—at home—I hoped. Quinn was hurting. I could feel it. But I wasn't the one to heal him. Not this time. A part of me regretted it. The old me—the one who needed to be needed. Not anymore. What Quinn was asking I could no longer give. I came to tell him about our son. I wouldn't let this moment of sweet memory make me forget that.

I stepped out of his arms. I needed the space, the distance between us. I looked into his confused eyes, and a sharp pain pierced my chest, knowing what I must say and the anguish my telling of it would cause. I'd run out of road. This was my stop.

"I didn't come here *just* because I care, Q. I came because—I—we—we have a son, Quinn. You and I."

His body flinched as if he'd been hit in the gut.

"What?" The tone was low, almost threatening, the same tone I'd heard him use against people I didn't want to remember.

I swallowed down the final knot of hesitation. Quinn never stuttered, and neither would I. Straight, no chaser. "We have a son. He's three–years–old. His name is Jamel. I was pregnant when you left and came back to New York, but I didn't find out until a week before I heard you were getting married. I didn't want it to interfere with that, Quinn."

He stared at me as if he didn't recognize me, then tapped a cigarette out of his pack and lit it.

I watched his jaw working as if he were chewing up his words before spitting them out at me.

"How did it happen? Better, *why* did it happen, Maxine?"

I raised my chin, unwilling to appear as vulnerable as I felt. "You know perfect well *how,* Quinn. Why? I've asked myself that question, too. It was an accident. I didn't *plan* to get pregnant, if that's what you're trying to say."

"It ain't about what I'm trying to say. It's about you. How do I even know it's mine? How do I know that you're not here, standin' in my face tellin' me some garbage, 'cause you caught me out here like this? Thinkin' I'm at some weak moment. Maybe you want somethin'. Is that the deal?"

"What could I possibly want from you?"

"Money. My name. Same things everybody else wants, Maxine."

I stared at him, as shocked as if he'd slapped me. Is that what he thought of me—so little?

"I've never asked or wanted anything from you as long as I've known you, Quinn Parker. Not a damned thing. So why start now?"

"You tell me. You're the one standin' here the day my wife is put in the ground tellin' me about—a baby." His eyes cinched and he stepped closer. "Why now? After all this time. Why today? To just mess with my head some more?"

For a moment I looked away. I'd risked everything to come here, to tell him what he should have been told long ago. Yet, even knowing that, the reality was, no time would have ever been the right time, and I told him so.

"Really?" he snapped, his voice laden with sarcastic bite. "How 'bout three years ago?"

He blew a cloud of smoke into the air, tossed the cigarette butt on the ground, and quickly lit another. I saw the slight tremor in his hands. My heart softened. I knew it couldn't have been easy for him, either.

"I probably shouldn't have—told you today. I should have told you as soon as I found out, no matter what was happening in your life, but I didn't. I didn't want to take the chance you would decide to come back to me only because of the baby. You left me, Quinn, not so much because you didn't love me. You just loved Nikita more. I understood that. As much as it hurt me, I understood. And I didn't want to do anything to jeopardize your finally being happy. How could I face you today, face myself, here and now, even under these circumstances and not tell you about our son? If I didn't, how many more years and how many more reasons would stand between us and this moment? I'm sorry. I can't undo it."

His eyes zeroed in on my face, and I felt it burn.

"You took the chance away from me, Maxine. The right to choose. Just like everything else has been taken from me." He cut his eyes at me, blew a puff of smoke in my direction. "What makes you any different from any other killer of dreams? Huh, Max?"

Then suddenly, he spread his arms like wings and began to turn in a macabre circle, his dreads whipping around his face, which was turned toward the sky. "Look where we are, Maxine. Look around you. A place of finality. Period. End of story. My sister and my wife are here." He stopped spinning and faced me. The muscles in his face tensed, his eyes filled to near overflowing. "And here *we* are, Maxine." His voice caught. "What does that say to you?"

He stamped out his cigarette, looked at me as if trying to memorize my face, then turned, and walked away across the slope until I lost sight of him.

It was then that I gave in to the storm cloud of emotions that had been swirling within and around me. My body began to quake with fear, resentment, pain, anger, and empathy. The torrent came then, pouring from my eyes almost strong enough to wash away the tide of sensations that continued to ebb and flow as I found my way back to Val's car. Almost.

By the time I reached the car, I'd reasonably pulled myself together.

Val started the engine as soon as I shut the car door. We pulled out of the parking space, me staring out of my window and Val looking straight ahead. Silence hung between us like the puffs of smoke Quinn had continually exhaled, until finally Val spoke.

"Are you all right?"

"Yeah. I think so. Or at least I will be."

"How's Quinn?"

My stomach tightened. "Angry, hurt, betrayed," I said on one long, flat note.

"How bad was it?"

"Pretty bad. But then I didn't actually think he'd break

out in song and carry me away so we could make a life together." Even as I said the words, there was a little echo in the back of my head, of my wishing that he would, or had at least cared enough to want to try, do the honorable thing.

When I confessed that to Val, she said something that truly hit a chord.

"It may not seem like it now, Max, but Quinn did the honorable thing. He honored his wife's memory by not simply running to you because of this bombshell you dropped. All of us wish our 'baby's daddy' would do the right thing. But be careful what you wish for. If Quinn had acted differently, treated you and this situation any differently than he did, you would have lost all respect for him as a man and as the natural father of your child."

"You're right, Val. I wouldn't have respected him, just as I wouldn't have respected myself if I'd betrayed what Taylor and I have. Seeing Quinn, hearing what he felt and feels for Nikita helped me clarify what I've always known. *That's* the way I feel about Taylor, Val—that relentless all consuming love, and a part of me would wither away without him. Seeing Quinn's love for his wife is a reflection of my own life, what I'm blessed to have.

"It was as if he were echoing the words that are in my heart for Ty." I turned and looked into the eyes of my friend. "That's why I came, Val. I needed to hear the words. I needed to say the words. There is no romp back to yesterday. Quinn belongs in the life of Maxine that doesn't exist anymore. My future is at home."

"Maybe after the shock of losing Nikita and then learning about Jamel has worn off and settled, after he finds a way to deal with both, the two of you can talk, find a way to work things out."

I rubbed my eyes. "Maybe. Today wasn't the day or the time for resolutions." Then one word rung in my head: Honor. Now it was time for me to do the honorable thing in my life. I could only hope that it wasn't too late.

TAYLOR

TEN

Only Time Will Tell

In the time Maxine was in New York I took the opportunity to do some real thinking about everything; about why I was with her; why it was so hard for her to tell me about Quinn; how easy it was for her to leave, and how I was ready to give up what we had because I didn't trust what we had anymore.

Staying with CJ and Tracy helped a lot, though—seeing them together, watching their marriage work—and at times I thought maybe that was what was wrong. Max and I lived together and loved together like a family, but we never made it legally official. Did that make it easier for her to go to Quinn, easier for me to walk out, because we didn't have a piece of paper telling us we were supposed to work it out through thick and thin, better or worse?

And why hadn't we? What were we afraid of? Afraid of a moment like this, one that would test the strength of our relationship to the fullest?

I thought about all that stuff, and even more that was scrambled like eggs in my head. Some things I had answers for. Others I didn't.

Looking out the window of the guest bedroom, I heard the distant rumble of a plane soaring overhead, and wondered if it was Maxine's plane.

She was due back today, and a lapping wave of unease rolled through me. What if she didn't come back? What if she and Quinn had decided to work things out between them? Then what?

I got up from the edge of the bed, moved across the olive–green carpeted floor and went downstairs. Maybe CJ was in the mood for a game of pool, and a beer. I sure didn't feel like listening to the questions in my head anymore.

When I got downstairs CJ was in his favorite spot, stretched out on the couch in front of the television. It was truly a wonder that he never put on a pound, when the couch was the first place he landed after a meal. And I couldn't get him to the gym for all the beer in a brewery.

"Hey, Man, whatsup?" he mumbled, covering his mouth with the back of his hand to stifle a yawn.

I walked farther into the room and flopped down on the recliner, stretching my legs out in front of me. Shrugging slightly, I asked him if he wanted to play a game of pool.

"The truth, or just what you wanna hear?"

"The truth."

"No."

I laughed. Guess I asked for it. "Come on, Man. Get your lazy butt up. I swear one of these days all that eating and sleeping is going to catch up with you."

"Don't hate me because I'm beautiful," he said in a perfect falsetto.

I sent the square paisley green pillow that was behind my back sailing across the room, catching him right in the head.

He tossed it on the floor. "Now, a game of one–on–one I might be interested in."

"Cool. Let's go."

He had a hoop that hung from above the garage door that unfortunately had seen better days. The net was non–existent, and the rim had rusted over time to a perfect shade of orange. Even though I beat him at this game every time, CJ swore the rusty rim brought him luck, and he refused to get a new one.

He went into the cluttered garage and hunted around the workbench and tools he never used, like discarded computers with their insides exposed and gardening equipment that Tracy insisted he put to good use every Saturday, until he unearthed the basketball.

The plap, plap sound of the ball hitting the concrete was rhythmic, like a heartbeat. There was some comfort in it, something familiar that I could usually hold on to. But even with sneakered feet hitting the pavement, the ball slamming against the garage wall, and our sweating bodies colliding, leaping, running, I felt unanchored, unsure of my step.

"One more basket," CJ wheezed, "and I got this game." He drove by me going straight for the hoop—up and in. Game over.

CJ bent from the waist, his hands braced on his knees, pulling air, it seemed, from the ground.

Finally he stood, sweat running down from his head like the Nile. I grabbed a towel from the back of the lawn chair and mopped my face. CJ approached.

"You do realize *your* butt just got whipped by *me*? You do realize that?" He snatched the towel from around my neck and ran it across his face and close–cut hair. "What day is today? 'Cause I sure have to write this down."

"Friday. Maxine's supposed to be back today."

"Hmm. Why suppose? You think she won't?"

"I don't know anymore, Man. I guess she's coming back.

At least for Jamel. I know she wouldn't leave him." I shrugged.

I felt him looking at me, but it was too hard to give it back, even to CJ. I didn't want him to see the fear in my eyes.

"I could use a beer. How 'bout it?" he asked, and I knew it was his way of telling me I could talk if and when I wanted to.

"Sounds good."

I trailed him into the house. "Where's Tracy?"

"Gone on a girl's night out or something. Don't expect her back for quite ... some ... time."

He took an ice cold bottle of Corona out of the fridge and handed it to me, then took another for himself. We walked back out into the living room and CJ put on a Thelonious Monk CD. "Round Midnight" blew effortlessly through the room.

I eased back in the recliner, took a long swallow of brew, closed my eyes, and let the abstract music carry me on its back. . . .

Maxine and I had danced to that music on one of our first dates after Jamel was born. It was a little out–of–the–way club where the food was from heaven and the music could plunge you into sin.

While we swayed to the music and I held her so close, I could feel her heart beat . . . beat in time with mine. Her soft scent, the feel of her skin, swam through my senses. I just felt her in every part of me. She was buried in my heart from the beginning—I couldn't have dug her out if I'd tried—and I didn't want to—ever. The power of those sensations, that moment of clarity, made me weak.

In those early months that we were together, we'd gone through what most couples never shared in a lifetime. I knew it was crazy, the way we'd found each other, the situation we were in. But it didn't matter. I loved her. Loved *her*—who she was, all that I knew she could be.

There were times back then when I experienced twinges of doubt about whether I was getting in over my head with Maxine—but then there were those times when we'd sit and talk about everything from grocery lists and literature, to music and the state of unrest in the world. Maxine had an opinion about everything. She challenged me with her mind, thrilled me with her body. Maybe she didn't have a bunch of college degrees like I did, and maybe she didn't grow up in a great neighborhood, but she was worldly in a real sense that couldn't be gained from lectures and diplomas, only from living and absorbing life. And she made everyone around her feel just as enthusiastic about things as she did.

I couldn't wait to get home at night just to be with her, hear about her day. And then when Jamel was born, just watching how she loved, nurtured, and cared for him made me see what a gift I'd been given in her.

So yes, I was afraid—afraid that everything that was my life, what I had become because of it, could disappear in a finger pop. If there was a lingering shadow in Maxine's heart that caused her to not feel as strongly about us as I did, then our forever would end. I didn't want to sound weak, like some soft pushover that's been whipped by a woman. I knew I was as much of a man as anyone out there. But I had feelings, too—feelings that ran deep, maybe too deep sometimes. That's why, I'd been so reluctant about getting involved with anyone again, after Karen, about turning my feelings inside out and exposing them to someone. But when I met Max, there was nothing I could do. I'd made a choice, taken a risk. Now I had to see what cards had been dealt to me.

"Want another brew, Ty?" CJ asked.

I opened my eyes, looking around at the here and now. "Naw. I'm good."

He leaned his head back against the arm of the couch. "What time is Max's flight?"

"Not sure." I took another swallow. The beer was starting to get warm.

"Want to call Marva and find out? Maybe meet Max at the airport?"

"Naw."

He was quiet for a moment. I could almost hear the stream of cool liquid slide down his throat.

Then his voice came to me. He sounded like a griot, an ancient African storyteller, ready to weave a tale—mine.

"You know when you and Maxine first got together I thought it was the worst mistake you'd ever made. I was set to dislike her, and I told her so. I wanted to give her a hard time. But I couldn't. She was real, and she cared for you, and I could see in your face that she made you happy, Man." He sat up slightly, leaned on his elbow. "It was *you* I couldn't really figure, and still don't quite understand.

"I mean, I know Maxine is fine and all, great personality, fun to be with, smart. But she was carrying another man's child, Brother." He shook his head in bewilderment. "What were you thinking? What was it about her that made you put yourself in that trick bag? I mean, did you ever think about all the consequences, especially about Jamel's dad? I just want to understand, Man. That's all."

The questions swarmed around me like killer bees, stinging all the exposed flesh. I tossed down the last of the Corona and stood. "I'm getting another beer. Want one?"

"Yeah."

While I was in the kitchen, I had an overwhelming impulse to walk out the back door and keep going so I wouldn't have to answer the questions—the same questions that played havoc with my head on many occasions. There were inklings of answers, but they were like smoke. I could almost see them, make out their shapes, but when I reached out to grab them, hold on and make them mine, they would vanish, slip from between my fingertips.

I didn't walk out. I went back. Maybe if I talked it out, heard my thoughts and uncertainties out loud, I could finally silence them.

I handed CJ his beer.

"Listen, Man, I was out of line. It's none of my business about you and Max. That's ya'll's thing. Just forget I asked, okay?"

Resting my arms on my thighs, I stared at my hands. "It's cool, Man. Hey, if you can't ask, who can?" I laughed a little to let him know it was okay. "I've been asking myself a lot of the same questions, CJ."

"Yeah. And—?"

I shrugged. "When I met Max it wasn't as if I was looking, or hungry for a woman. It was nothing she said, or anything special that she did. I just felt as if I'd awakened from a deep sleep when she looked at me." I took a short sip of beer, trying to gather my thoughts so they'd make sense.

"Most of my life I never felt as if I belonged, you know, moving from one family to the next. I didn't have any roots, no history. I don't think anyone can really understand how important that is unless they've experienced it. People take family and being a part of it for granted." I shook my head. "If they only knew. *Humph.* Karen was the first woman who seemed to really care about me—or at least, I convinced myself that she did. I opened myself up to her. It was like I needed to, you know, have somebody understand what was going on inside me. I told her how my life had been. I guess I was hoping that she'd feel even more deeply for me, want to make me a part of her life, belong to her."

I stood. "Oh, Man, I know this sounds crazy, like some soft kid or something." I glanced at CJ.

"Listen, Brother, anything you say to me is cool. You got to know that. What's said here stays here. It's not gonna make me think any less of you, if that's what's on your mind. I mean, I know you've been through a lot, from some of the stuff you've told me. We go way back, Brother.

But I know you still have a heavy load on you. If you want to kick it, fine. If not, I'll understand.''

I nodded, slowly sat back down, and let the words, the visions free flow. "I remember one night Karen and I were laying up. We'd just made love, and she asked me where I grew up. I didn't want to tell her at first, but she started stroking my head, talking all soft, telling me I could tell her anything.

She asked me, "how bad could it be?"

"Bad enough. I lived in more places than I can remember, most of them short–term. It was hard to place little black boys. That's what I always heard the social workers say," I'd told her.

"I didn't want to sound bitter, you know, CJ? But I was. What was the fear of little black boys? Was the fear that if they were cared about and loved—that they might actually grow up into thriving, functioning black men who wanted more than just a slow death?"

"Did you say that to her?"

"Naw. I wasn't sure she'd really understand. I didn't really understand it myself at the time. So anyway, we were lying there, and I started telling her about this one place I lived.

"I was about twelve when I got sent to live with Mrs. Long. She was really nice. There were three other kids, two boys and a girl. Mark, Jason, and Janice. They were all foster kids, too. Mark had lived with Mrs. Long since he was a year old. His mother died of a crack overdose, and he was born addicted. He was about ten, but he looked about six. And he talked real slowly sometimes, like his battery was running low. Jason and Janice were brother and sister. They were both younger than me, too.

"I stayed with Mrs. Long for about four years. I thought she was going to adopt me. She was good to me. Always looked out for me, made sure I ate, had clean clothes, did my homework. She was the one who first showed me how to care, and what it felt like to be cared about.''

"Did she have any of her own kids?" CJ asked.

"No. She told me she couldn't have any, so she decided to make sure that kids who didn't have a home would have one with her.''

"Why didn't she just adopt?"

"I think she wanted to spread her mothering to as many as she could. She couldn't do that with just one or two adopted kids.

"Karen said that maybe Mrs. Long didn't want to be a real mother, with permanent responsibility, that if she ever got tired of it, she could just send the kids back. She said it wasn't that easy when you're a real mother. I angled my head and looked at her. She was staring up at the ceiling, totally detached. And a strange feeling came over me, a shift in my stomach. I didn't want to believe that about Mrs. Long. I didn't want to believe that what she gave me was superficial, temporary, or for the money. But as much as I tried to shake it, the thought was planted in my head. And that old unease, that feeling of rootlessness, slipped in again.

"I tried to fight it, CJ, by giving everything I had to Karen—material, mental, emotional, physical. It was as if I needed to prove something to myself and to her, hoping that she would see that I was worthy of something deep and permanent. But it was as if the more I gave her, the more distant she became.

"One night, I came in from work. It had been hot as hell all day, and I couldn't wait to get in the shower. Karen was stretched out on the bed reading a magazine. She barely noticed me when I came in. She briefly glanced up from what she was reading.

" 'Hey, Babe,' I said, 'how was your day?' I loosened my tie and unbuttoned my shirt.

" 'Fine.'

" 'Nothing special?'

" 'No.'

" 'I'm going to take a shower.'

" *'Hmm.'*

"When I came back out she was in her nightgown, lying on top of the covers, with the lights turned down. Now, a nightgown was something Karen never wore, but I thought it was just something new. I smiled. Maybe she had been acting the way she did when I first came in so she could surprise me. I got in beside her and pulled her next to me. I felt her body stiffen beneath the silky fabric.

" 'What's wrong, Karen?' I asked.

" 'Nothing. I just don't feel like it,' " she said and turned on her side, giving me her back.

" 'Talk to me, Karen. What's with you lately?'

" 'You really want to know?'

" 'Yes. What is it?' "

"She sat up and glared at me. 'I got rid of your baby today.'

"All of the air rushed out of me at once. I sat up and tried to focus on her face, but my head felt like it was spinning, and my heart was racing.

" 'What are you saying—you got rid of my baby?'

" 'I was pregnant this morning. I'm not now.'

"I grabbed her arm. I wanted to slam her into the wall. 'What the hell are you talking about? Why didn't you tell me you were pregnant? How could you do something like that?' "

" 'I didn't want you to try to talk me out of it. Not that it would have mattered.' "

"I couldn't believe what she was saying. She wasn't making sense to me. All the words jumbled together in my head, and I started to feel sick.

" 'Why, Karen? Tell me why you did it.'

" 'I can't have a baby from somebody who doesn't know who he is.'

"The words hit me like a bevy of roundhouse punches, and I felt myself sinking. My own words to her had come back to haunt me. *Somebody who doesn't know who he is.* I'd opened the doors to this woman who I thought loved me, told her my deepest hurts and fears, and she used them against me.

"I got up out of the bed, found my clothes in the dark and got dressed.

" 'I'm going out for a few hours,' I told her, 'I don't want you or your things here when I get back.' "

Blinking, I put my empty beer bottle on the coffee table and dared to take a look at CJ, not sure what I'd see. The understanding in his eyes slowed the rapid pumping of my heart.

"Damn, Man, I'm sorry," CJ said. "I never knew it was like that."

"It's not something I was ever too eager to talk about. I mean, you knew some of it, but—"

"Hey, you were better off without her. Woman like that, no telling when she would have shown her true colors. Better sooner than later."

I got up and stretched, walked across the living room, and checked the collection of CDs. I picked *Sarah Vaughan's Greatest Hits,* the old classics, and put it on the player. For a few moments I stood there with my eyes closed, letting the sultry riffs of her voice wash over me.

"Yeah. For a long time, I totally distrusted women." I started moving back across the room and sat back down. "Wouldn't let anyone get close to me. I just felt that if anyone really got to know me they'd eventually feel the same way about me that Karen did. I mean, I was believing it. Who knew what was dangling from my family tree? And I went on like that for years. Stayed emotionally distant. I couldn't get hurt if I didn't get my feelings involved."

"Yeah. The ice man."

We both looked at each other with half smiles of knowing.

"But when I met Maxine, something happened to me. I knew from the moment I met her that she was a genuinely good person, a kindhearted person. Believe me, it scared me. I finally wanted to trust again."

"Was that all the reason you needed to stay with her when she told you she was pregnant?"

"The first reaction I had was shock. Then a sudden feeling of loss, CJ. I felt like I'd lost her, and I knew I didn't want to. I needed her in my life. That's all I could think about at the time. Damn the risks, the consequences. It took a while for me to realize why I was willing to accept the situation. And it was Karen's words that came back to haunt me. *I* could be a father without the risks."

"Did Maxine know this?"

I shook my head. "No. Not at first. I wasn't really sure myself. But as time moved on, I began to understand why I'd done it. I wanted to redeem myself somehow, but at the same time I didn't have to risk her telling me she didn't want a child of mine, because of who I *wasn't*. That was already taken care of. And I could still be a father and have the woman I was in love with."

CJ looked at me for a long time. I guess he didn't know what to say. "But what about now? I mean, do you still feel the same way about Jamel—that he's just a risk free investment?"

I heard the edge in his voice, but he knew how I felt about Jamel.

"I couldn't love him any more if he were my own son, Man. Believe that. What I didn't realize was that in trying to avoid risks I was taking an even bigger one. I chose to be where I am. I chose to be his dad, to be with his mom. I chose to love them. And any time you make choices you take a risk of consequences. And this consequence is a major one. I'm *not* his dad. And his father could decide he wants his son—and Maxine."

"But you said you trusted Maxine. If you trust her, then you have to trust that she's going to do the right thing by you and Jamel."

"That's what I'm holding on to, Man. It's what I'm holding on to."

ELEVEN

Nowhere to Run

CJ and I kicked it for several more hours—skipping back and forth from one topic to the next, light chatter—but it always came back to Max and me, and what I was prepared to do, what it was that I wanted.

"How come you think she didn't tell you when she got the call?" CJ asked.

"That's something that's been bothering me the most. Why would she be afraid to tell me if she had every intention of doing the right thing?"

"Hey, maybe she was just worried you'd *think* the wrong thing. I mean, it is kind of an awkward situation."

"Yeah. I guess. But her not telling me, CJ, getting the ticket without saying a word, is what caused all the trouble." I got up and started a slow pace across the hardwood floor. "This whole thing gave me a deja vu moment of what went down between me and Karen. When Maxine got distant with me, didn't want me to touch her, all I could think was—*not again.*"

"Oh, Man. Listen, everything is going to work out. Max isn't Karen. You two have a lot going on between you, something worth fighting for."

I thought about that as I drove home after finally deciding I wanted to be there when Maxine got in. His words stayed with me, wise and unshakable.

I probably should have called Marva, as CJ suggested, found out what time Max's flight arrived, but a part of me wasn't prepared for anything I didn't want to hear.

The early evening was clear for a change. A light breeze blew in from the bay, bringing the scent of salt water with it. With twilight gradually approaching, the rolling streets became a twinkling phantasm as lights began to fill the dimming sky.

On so many nights like this one, Maxine and I took late night drives with Jamel tucked in the backseat fast asleep. We had no particular destination in mind, just wanted to spend time together, seeing what we could see, talking about our day.

I remembered one night. Jamel was about a year old. . . .

I'd just gotten in from work, and Maxine had prepared a picnic dinner for us.

"I thought we could celebrate the anniversary of our first date," she said, greeting me at the door with a long, slow kiss.

"I like the sound of that," I breathed against her mouth, pulling her closer. "We could start celebrating right here, you know."

She laughed and gently tugged my bottom lip with her teeth. She knew that made me crazy.

"Now, that would take all of the anticipation out of it." She ran her hands down my back. "Why don't you get changed, and we can go."

"What about Jamel?"

She gave me a coy look, tipping her head to the side. "Marva said we could drop him by her house if we wanted to spend some private time together, undisturbed. But I thought, if it's okay with you, we could bring him with us."

"Baby, whatever you want. Having him with us will help me to behave myself."

"Oh, yeah? It never helped before."

"Very funny." That much was true. There were many nights when he woke up and Max put him in the bed with us to get him back to sleep. I knew once he got the hang of it that he was running a game on both of us, but I loved it. I loved watching her with him. The gentleness was such a turn on that we would wind up making love with him right beside us.

That night was no different, even better. We found a beautiful little spot tucked away right off the beach. The sky overhead was pitch dark, with a sprinkling of stars.

"Max, I've been living here all my life and I didn't know anything about this place," I said, lifting Jamel out of his carseat.

She laughed, that soft, mischievous laugh that always made me feel warm inside. "I told you my scavenging would pay off one of these days."

She stepped up to me and kissed me, and Jamel rubbed my face with a damp hand and flashed me a toothless smile. *This is what it's about,* I thought. *This is what it feels like to be a part of a family, to be loved and be a part of something that matters.*

"I love you, Maxine."

"And I love you. Always."

Jamel began to squirm, and we both laughed.

"We love you, too, buddy," I said, and kissed the top of his head.

After we'd laid out everything and gotten Jamel settled we stretched out on the blanket, nibbling on the food and each other.

"This past year has been great, Maxine. Every minute."

She looked at me the way she did sometimes—with amazement in her eyes—almost as if she couldn't believe that this was her life, that she was loved and cared about, that we were a family.

From what she'd shared with me about her relationship with Quinn, she had always been holding her breath, expecting any minute that things would fall apart. There was a part of her that still harbored those fears.

"You have me, Maxine. You're in my heart. I want you to believe that."

She hesitated a beat, bit down on her lip like she did sometimes. "I know. I do. It's just that sometimes it's hard for me to accept that everything is actually working out, that we love each other."

"Tell me again," I teased.

She arched her right eyebrow. "Tell you what?"

"You know—how crazy you are about me."

"Oh, boost your ego?"

"Exactly."

She laughed, then touched her lips to mine. "I love you, Taylor Collins. And I feel truly blessed that you're in my life."

"Now, *that's* what a man likes to hear." I pulled her to me, brushed a crumb from her bottom lip with the tip of my finger, saw her eyelids flutter closed.

Hmm. Kissing Maxine was like a slice of heavenly pie, light, sweet, soft enough to make me think it was just my imagination. Made me want more and more just to test it, be certain it was real. And it was, just like the silky feel of her skin beneath my hands, skin that compelled me to touch it, stroke it, so that I could hear her soft moans as she heated to my touch.

But it wasn't just the feel of her skin, or the taste of her lips. Being inside of, and part of, Maxine was an experience that cannot be explained or defined.

Every time we were together we seemed to climb to greater heights, until it wasn't just a total physical experience, it was spiritual.

As we lay on the blanket, with Jamel fast asleep beside us, whispering, caressing each other, little by little removing our clothing, I couldn't have imagined what that union would be like.

When I saw her bare, dark skin slowly emerge, felt the soft roundness of her breasts in my hands, the flat stomach with the faint lines across her waist and hips, the dark, coarse tuft of hair, and those incredible legs that spread and welcomed me, I knew that night would be different.

I was sure of it the instant I felt myself ease inside her, in the way her body arched, in the jolt that shot through me when I felt her insides tighten and call me home.

I knew I'd left my body, because there was no way on earth that anything could feel the way Maxine made me feel. I tumbled in love with her over and over again with each rise and fall, every whimper, every stroke, every touch.

When it was over and we were holding each other, I could tell she was crying. I eased up and looked down at her. "What's the matter, Baby? What's wrong?"

She sniffed and turned her head.

"Maxine, talk to me."

"It's just . . . you're so good to me, Ty. Good for me, too, and no one could ask for a more caring father for Jamel. And—I guess what always gets to me is that you didn't have to do this. You didn't have to be with me. You could have walked out and never looked back when I told you about Jamel, but you didn't. Why? Why didn't you walk away?"

Before that time, I'd never dared to fully answer the very same question I'd asked myself. The question would form: why did you do this? And as the answers began to materialize like a figure emerging from the mists, I would push it aside, make it go back.

Maybe I didn't really want the answer to become full-blown, because then I'd have to deal with it and everything it meant.

But lying there with her, still feeling the aftershock of our lovemaking, her looking at me wanting and deserving an answer, I knew the time had come.

"Because it was safe," I finally said.

"Safe?"

"It's hard to explain, Max. For a long time there was a part of me that didn't feel I deserved to be a parent—a father. I've asked myself time and again if what I did was selfish, self–serving. Was I being a coward by not dealing with my real issues—my *lack* of being? Was I being fair to you, to Jamel?"

She touched my cheek. "Why, Taylor? You're wonderful."

I told her about Karen and what she'd said and done, how it had left me feeling inadequate.

"And then I met you, and fell in love, really in love for the first time. Believe me, it was the hardest thing I've ever had to deal with when you told me you were carrying another man's child. It tore me apart. But I realized that even with that I didn't want to lose you. I couldn't. When I thought about the baby I knew I could never be accused of giving it bad genes, not giving it roots—but at the same time I could still be a father, love the child, and still have you."

She looked at me for a long time, as if she were trying to make out who I was in the dark. Maybe she was. Maybe she was seeing me for the first time, through new eyes. The idea that the vision would become distorted, unappealing, suddenly scared me. Scared me to think that once I'd let my defenses down, shared my inner self that I'd kept hidden even from myself, she would walk away from the image.

"Funny how and why we got together, Taylor," she'd said, curling closer to me. "I guess I was pretty much like

you most of my life. Although I had a family, I never felt
as if I was really cared about. My mom was so busy trying
to get my dad's attention, that she pretty much ignored
me as much as my dad did. We both idolized my dad, and
he disregarded us both. I suppose I spent most of my life
looking for "daddy" and "daddy's love."

"And you thought you found it in Quinn?"

I felt her nod her head. "He was distant, mysterious in
his inaccessibility. That was the charm, the allure. And
then reality hit—Jamel. And it was no longer a matter of
chasing a girlhood dream. I had to grow up and see my
life and myself for what they really were. When I met you,
I finally realized that I was worthy of being loved, and
capable of giving it back. I didn't need to accept crumbs
of affection. You taught me that."

I pulled her closer and my heart filled.

"You said that for a long time there was a part of you
that felt inadequate, not worthy," she finally said. "Do you
still feel that way?"

"No. Not anymore. But it took being with you, being a
part of your life, helping to raise Jamel, feeling needed
and loved. That's what changed it for me. You changed it
for me, Maxine. You're the other half of who I am, Baby.
The part that I've spent most of my life searching for."

I knew I was probably sounding like some whipped
puppy, but I needed her to know the impact of how having
her in my life had changed me, as having me had changed
her. And all the other things—the baggage of our pasts—
didn't matter.

They hadn't.

Until now. . . .

I pulled up in front of our house. It was dark, and with
the darkness came a heavy sadness that sat on my chest. I
didn't want to come home—to this home, any home—
and not have Maxine in it. Whatever the deal was, whatever
happened with her and Quinn in New York, we would

work it out. We had to. There was too much at stake. And I wasn't letting go easily. Not without a fight. Jamel was my son, Maxine was my woman.

I wasn't sure how the deck was going to be played, but I had the trump hand. This was *my* family.

MAXINE

TWELVE

Over The Rainbow

When I saw Jamel running toward me at the airport, all the anxiety, all the angst of the past twenty–four hours, disappeared like clothing being peeled away during a summer heat wave. I was home, where I was supposed to be. This trip was a metamorphis—a time for change. It was about facing who I was, who we all were. I could only pray that I hadn't lost my man in the process of finding my way back.

Jamel grabbed me around my thighs and I scooped him up in my arms, lovingly hugging him to me, inhaling the baby scent of him. My chest tightened, and my eyes stung.

"Hey, baby." I plopped kisses all over his face. "Mommy missed her boy. Been good?"

"Yes."

"Are you sure?" I wiggled my finger in his side, and he giggled and started to squirm.

"We going home?"

"Yes. We're going home."

"Hey, Girl," Marva said as she approached, a questioning look in her eyes.

"Hi. Thanks for coming, especially for taking care of Jamel."

"We had a ball. Right, Mel–Mel."

"Yes." He grinned. "I'm hungry, Mommy."

"What else is new? Let's get you home so you can eat."

"Frosted Flakes?"

I pinched his nose. "Whatever you want."

"You want to go straight home, or do you want to come to my place?" Marva asked as we pulled out of the parking lot, winding our way around the maze of the airport.

There was a sudden urgency in me, and I realized it had been building since I'd left New York. Sure, I could take the easy way out and go to Marva's house, put off the inevitable a while longer. But I hadn't taken the easy way out since this whole thing began. I didn't want to start now.

It was all about choices. I finally made the conscious choice to confront the truth and myself. And because of that I knew my commitment to Taylor was unshakable. But in order for me to fully understand the power of that commitment I had to totally discard the debris of the past, and everything I fantasize it as being. I had to experience the pain of separation. This was my reality.

Strangely enough I didn't just feel relief that it was finally done. I felt pleased with myself, because for the first time I'd taken a true stand, saw something all the way through even though the anguish of my actions had pierced my soul, that of Taylor's and of Quinn's. What saddens me most is that I am responsible for the disarray, the hurt and confusion. By not making a real decision three years ago, by not taking a stand, the decision was made for all of us. I relinquished control of the situation and as a result we

all were forced to deal with the consequences that life
dealt.

But I made a commitment at that gravesite to do what
was right, to honor my relationship with my man, to honor
my son's father by not backing away from the truth and
to finally be the complete woman that my son and Taylor
deserved. All that I could be. Dre was wrong. I could com-
mit. At last.

"I need to go home. Face whatever is there. Or whatever
isn't."

She nodded and patted my thigh in understanding.

"Have you heard from him?" I asked.

"No."

My heart pounded. I turned my head, stared out the
window. The cars flashing by in a kaleidoscopic array of
colors, the lights from the city blinking like cat's eyes in
the dark, were all part of my peripheral senses. I saw it all,
but didn't. To imagine that Taylor would not be a central
part of my and Jamel's life made me feel that I was no
longer a part of the scene, but an outsider looking in—
someone who didn't belong in the picture, the wrong
puzzle piece. Whatever it took, I'd make the pieces fit—
securely.

"How did things go with you and—"

A flash of our encounter at the cemetery jolted my
senses. I turned toward her.

"Not well."

"Did you at least work out anything about—?" She
angled her head toward the back where Jamel was strapped
into the carseat.

"No. He was so angry. Maybe angry isn't the word. So
betrayed. He said I was a killer of dreams, just like everyone
else."

"Oh, Max." She rubbed my hand, which was clenched
in a fist. "Don't take it to heart. He's hurting, and he

needed to strike out, that's all. I'm sure he didn't really mean that. It had to be a shock.''

"I tried to tell him I did it because I didn't want to interfere with his finally having happiness."

"And?"

"He said I took the chance away from him. I made the decision for him."

Marva was quiet for a moment, concentrating, it seemed, on the stop and go freeway traffic. I peeked behind me, and Jamel had fallen asleep.

"When I decided to marry Brent," she began, and I could hear her voice traversing back and pushing aside the thicket of images from the past, clearing a pathway to what needed exposing. "I knew it was a decision that would alter the rest of my life. It would change the way I fit into my family, the way I was seen by my so-called friends. Everything that was familiar to me, that I'd come to rely on, would change.

"The night before we'd decided to go to my parents and tell them our plans, Brent and I were up most of the night, just talking, holding hands, giving each other support. He had a small loft at the time, not too far from the coast." She smiled. "Sometimes you could hear the waves surging against the shore. We were stretched out on his bed. All the lights were out, and the moon tossed us into silhouettes against the white walls.

" 'I wish there were some other way,' he said to me. 'I know how much your folks mean to you, Marva.'

"I turned on my side and touched my lips to his. 'Yes, my family is important, and I know this is going to hurt me because I hurt them. But, Brent, what I feel for you will fill those gaps and ease any pain. I'm not going to lose you because 'they' tell me to let you go. They have to deal with their class issues, and snobbery. They don't have to live inside my heart. You do.'

"He looked at me, and I could see his eyes fill seconds before he pulled me into his arms.

" 'There's nothing we can't do together, Marva. Nothing. As long as I know you love me, I'll take on the world to make you happy.'

"It was hard at first, Maxine. Really hard," she confessed. "At times I felt like giving up. I missed the closeness I had with my mother and father, my sisters, but you know what? Slowly, one by one, they all did a complete turnaround. Now they adore Brent, and they realize that I didn't take anything away from the family when I married him. I brought them a gift."

I understood the underlying message hidden in the folds of her story. And the message was simple—honor my decision, my choices, my relationship, by standing up for them. And if Quinn chose at some point to realize what I was offering him, I would have to be ready to accept it. Taylor was our gift, a blessing to both my son and myself, and I had no intention of relinquishing our gift.

The car slowed, then came to a full stop. We were in front of my house. My stomach crescendoed like the last high note on the scales which seemed to reverberate through my chest and pound in my head.

The lights were on. Ty's car was parked next to mine in the driveway, as it always was. He was back. I silently prayed that it was for good.

"You want me to come in with you?" Marva asked.

"No. I don't think so. I need to do this."

"Should I take Jamel with me so you and Ty can have some time together—to talk?"

I turned and looked at my sleeping baby. "We need to deal with this as a family. And Jamel is a major part of it. But thanks. I appreciate it."

I eased Jamel out of his carseat. He whimpered for a second, then curled up in my arms and went back to sleep.

Marva took my overnight bag from the trunk and walked us to the front door.

I fished my key out of my jacket pocket while balancing Jamel in my other arm.

"Here, let me get that." Marva took the key from my hand and unlocked the door.

"Thanks," I mumbled over my racing heart.

We all stepped inside, and the aroma of barbecued chicken baking in the oven greeted us. A swell of emotion rushed from my chest and knotted in my throat.

"Are you going to be all right? I can stay a while," she said in a pseudo whisper.

"No. You go ahead. I'll be fine. Thanks for everything, Marva."

"Okay. But you call me in the morning. I'll be home all day."

I nodded and watched her leave.

Taking a deep breath of resolve, I walked toward the kitchen. I stood in the archway for several moments, simply watching Taylor. He was preparing dinner for us, I realized with a pang, and wondered what that really meant.

Seeing him there doing what he did so often brought a sense of comforting peace. It had always been one of the many ways in which he showed me he cared and was thinking about me—about us—wanting to make the end of my day as relaxing and pleasant as possible. My soul filled with the hope that the damage I'd caused wasn't beyond repair.

"Hi," I whispered.

Slowly he turned toward me as if he knew I was there and had just been waiting for me to speak. His expression was soft and inviting. I held Jamel a bit tighter, and could feel my heart pounding against his small body.

"Hope you're hungry," he said, his words almost hesitant over a shaky smile. "Dinner will be ready soon."

I swallowed. "Can I help with anything?"

"Always."

"I'll put Jamel to bed and be right back down."

He nodded.

As I gently undressed Jamel and put him beneath his covers, all I could think was: *Please let me do this right. Let my heart speak.* The litany ran over and over again in my brain until it became a silent chant as I returned downstairs.

I eased alongside Taylor and gently took the knife from his hand—our fingers slightly brushing—and we looked at each other, momentarily caught in a tableau of shared memories. I finished dicing the tomatoes for the salad, and he turned away.

"I wasn't sure what time you'd be back. I was hoping to have everything finished," Taylor said, not looking at me.

"I should have called."

"Is Jamel still asleep?"

"Uh, huh," I mumbled.

He opened the oven door to check on the food. "Just a few more minutes."

"How long have you been home?"

"A couple of hours. I was at CJ's."

"Oh." I tossed the tomatoes in with the spinach, then diced the mushrooms. "How is he—and Tracy?"

"Fine. Tracy was on a girls' night out."

"So you and CJ had some guy time—to talk?"

"Yeah. We talked. Some."

"Oh." I took two sets of dishes out of the china cabinet and set them on the table, then busied myself with utensils and glasses.

"Do you want to wake Jamel so he can eat?" he asked.

"No. Marva fed him already."

"She's a good friend."

"Yes. She is."

"It's good to have friends—real ones—that stick with you, that you can talk with no matter what."

I turned away from the table, and he was staring at me. My stomach fluttered. "I think we're both lucky like that—to have good friends we can depend on."

His gaze ran over me from top to bottom, holding me in place.

"Dinner's ready." He turned away and took the tray of chicken from the oven.

We sat at the butcher block table—the same table that we'd sat on opposite sides of for the past three years. The sights and scents were the same. The sounds of the house, the traffic that flowed outside, all wrought feelings of the familiar. Yet everything was different—changed.

I knew that Taylor and I had reached a new crossroads in our relationship, and if we dared to walk that path together we would be all the stronger for it.

We ate in silence. The clink of silver against china, the sounds of glass tapping wood, were all appetizers for the real main course. I knew that this atmosphere of normalcy barely acknowledged the true nature of what vibrated back and forth between us. The act of picking up a fork, drinking from a glass, helped to maintain the tenuous balance, but I knew it couldn't last. At some point what was on our minds and in our hearts would be shared, just like the meal—prepared and served when it was ready.

Taylor raised his glass to his lips. "How was your trip?"

I swallowed a mouthful of wild rice. "Difficult."

He nodded. "For you, or for him?" He put down his glass and looked at me.

"For both of us."

I saw a muscle under his right eye jump. *"Hmm.* How's Val?"

"Doing well. I saw quite a few people from the old neighborhood."

"Must have felt good being back home again."

"This is my home, Ty. With you and Jamel."

"Is it?"

I heard the question. More than that, I heard the pain in his voice, and knew what he was *really* asking me—What choice had I made, and was he that choice?

I put down my fork. "Ty . . . I know how I went about all this was wrong. I should have been up front with you from the beginning—trusted you to understand."

"Why didn't you, Max? Why?"

"I was afraid."

"Of what? Of me?"

"Afraid of the feelings that resurfaced for Quinn when I got the call from Val."

The silence that slammed down between us reverberated like a shout in the Grand Canyon.

"I see," he finally said, and he got up, taking his plate to the sink. "And what are those feelings, Maxine?" He kept his back to me.

"Only pieces of dreams, Ty. I realized that before the plane landed in New York. When I thought about what we have, you and I, and what I *thought* I had with Quinn, there was no question in my mind or in my heart. But I had to go, Ty. I had to see and feel it for myself. Put it to rest once and for all. I didn't understand it then, but when I chose to make my life without Quinn, not tell him about Jamel, I let my inaction make my decision for me. That was the behavior of a naive girl. I'm no longer in that place, Ty."

"Are you sure this is what you want, Maxine? Or do you only want it because he didn't want you—again. Just like before?"

The impact of his question sucked the air from my lungs and shook me to my core, opening up a dark chasm of hurt that I'd successfully pushed into the caverns of my mind.

"I was foolish, Ty. I made the same mistake twice—trying to think for someone other than myself, taking the choice out of their hands, out of mine by not deciding. I

did it to Quinn three years ago, and then I did it to you."
I stood, knowing that what would be said now would determine where Taylor and I would be later.

"But everything I did, I did because I cared. I thought I was doing what was right. What was best. Maybe I didn't lie, but I backed away from the truth. I won't do that anymore. I love you. I love what we have, and the life we've made. And yes, it hurt me to know that Quinn chose Nikita over me, but that was then, a lifetime ago. I choose you. Now, and for as long as you'll have me."

He crossed the short distance between us and stood in front of me. "Are you sure?"

"I've never been more certain of anything in my life."

"You hurt me, Maxine. I need you to know that. You hurt me by not trusting me enough to know that I would stand by you against anything, in your corner to the last round. You're my world, woman. You and that little boy up there. But I'll walk away and not look back if there's any doubt in your mind about us."

I cupped his face in my hands and looked into his eyes, praying that he could see deep into my heart. "There's no doubt, Taylor. None. And I promise you I'll spend the rest of my life making sure you know that. Forgive me, Baby. I'm so sorry."

I felt tears roll down my face, then become absorbed against the soft cotton of his shirt as I found myself in the strong safety of his arms. The sobs rocked me then, exorcising the fears, the doubts, the pain washing them out and away—freeing me to love my man totally and completely, the way he deserved to be loved.

"You've been gone too long, Girl. I missed you," he murmured against my mouth an instant before his possessed mine.

We clung together, holding, stroking, whispering what was in our hearts. Nothing before that moment, the here and now, mattered. It was about us—Taylor and I and what we felt for each other and always had from the beginning.

I heard the low groan come from deep in his throat and it spread through me, heated me like a shot of warm brandy. I couldn't get close enough, even though our bodies seemed fused and our hands and mouths explored all exposed flesh.

"This is crazy," he whispered in my ear before running his tongue along the cord of my neck.

My legs wobbled, and I held him tighter.

"It's crazy to want someone as much as I want you, Maxine." He opened the buttons of my blouse. "Every day. All the time." He pulled off my blouse and tossed it on the floor. "You're beautiful. You know that?"

I couldn't answer. My words were transformed in my throat, ready to emerge as a moan when his tongue sought the crest of my breasts and his fingers—the tender tips—stroked them until they rose and hardened to his touch.

Every nerve ending in my body exploded in unison when he unzipped my jeans and his deft fingers stroked the soft folds of my sex, sliding over the welcoming wetness, teasing the tiny bud until it flowered, beating as rapidly as my heart.

All at once sensations moved in horizontal and vertical lines, crisscrossing through me like intricate circuits all electrified, setting off tiny charges that pulsed, tingled, vibrated.

I felt my thighs bump against the back of the table edge as I stepped out of my pants and relieved Taylor of his.

He lifted me from the waist and raised me like a delicate piece of china onto the table. The look in his eyes singed my bare flesh as they roved over my body while he removed the rest of my clothes.

"You're incredible, Max" he said, his breath like a hot breeze against my throat.

"You make me feel incredible every time you look at me."

He pulled my hips toward him, forcing me to brace my hands behind me.

"Touch me like you want me," he urged in a ragged whisper.

And I did. The sensation of granite sheathed in flesh of satin, throbbing to my touch, filled me as always with a sense of awesome power.

When the hard tip of him pushed against my soft, yielding opening, filling my body, my mind, my soul—I knew I was truly home. It was sweet and raw, urgent and slow, searching, conquering, and submitting, all right there on the table where we'd just shared our meal, our thoughts, and now shared our bodies.

Somehow—weak, giddy, and totally satisfied—we stumbled, tiptoed, and half carried each other up the stairs to our bedroom.

"*Ssh,*" Taylor whispered at the top of the landing, covering my mouth with a long kiss to stifle my laughter. "You'll wake Jamel."

I felt drugged, high on love, floating, and I wanted everyone to know how happy I was, and how loved I felt.

"Okay. Okay," I whispered back as we went into our room. As much as I might have wanted the world to know how good I felt, I really didn't want them to know just then, not when the opportunity for a repeat so readily presented itself.

I slid under the covers, and Taylor was right behind me. Damn, it felt good to be in his arms again, to feel secure. To think that only days ago I'd risked what we had, everything we'd built, just to confirm what a part of me always knew. This was where I belonged, and I'd almost lost everything. The thought sent a chill up my spine.

"You okay, Baby? Cold?" He pulled the sheet up over my shoulder.

I could have just said yes, or nothing at all, but if Taylor and I were going to continue to survive as a couple, it had to be about honesty. No more hiding from the truth.

"I could have lost you, Ty." I moved closer to him, needing to feel his heartbeat. "My inability to confront painful decisions, by making them through avoidance, colored most of my life. I know I'm so much more than that now. Because of you and because of me and the woman I've finally become." I stroked his cheek. "I'll never let anyone or anything come between us again. I promise you that. I love you, Ty. For as long as you'll let me."

Like a whisper in the dark he touched his lips to mine.

"I needed to hear that, Max. I need to know that you want me as much as I want you, and that we're in this relationship together."

"We are."

For a while we were quiet, simply holding each other, rediscovering each other in a way, listening to the rhythms of our breathing and the beat of our hearts.

When we did begin to talk again that night, Taylor asked me about my conversation with Quinn, what he'd said, and how he'd reacted. I told him as truthfully as possible, leaving nothing out, not even the pain I'd felt when Quinn asked me how he could know Jamel was his.

"The day is going to come Maxine, after the smoke and the shock clears, when he is going to do more than just walk away. Quinn is going to want to see his son. From everything you've ever told me about him, from the articles I've read about him, he's not the type of man to walk away from responsibility. If he took on taking care of himself and his twin sister at sixteen, there's nothing to stop him from coming for Jamel, bringing his name, his money, his biological connection, and whatever else he thinks is necessary to have a role in Jamel's life. No matter what happens, we—you and I—must think of Jamel first, and what's best for him. Whatever that means."

As I listened to the words that had rested unspoken in my heart waiting to be uttered, a fear unlike any I'd ever known mushroomed inside of me. But I knew I was ready to face it.

Ty pulled me closer. "And he *will* come."

QUINN

THIRTEEN

The Road Back

The days turned into mindless, empty weeks after Niki's funeral. I wandered around my own house lost, not really sure what I was doing, where I was going. There was an emptiness in the house and in the pit of my belly that echoed with every breath I took.

Some days I thought I was going over the edge—no doubt. I would suddenly think I heard her voice, her laughter, and at the strangest times I could smell her scent all around me. And then the realization would hit me that she wasn't there. Gone forever.

Nothing mattered to me. Not the lectures from Mrs. Finch, the phone calls and visits from Nick, Remy, and even T.C., my old running buddy from the neighborhood. I just didn't care anymore—about anything.

Maybe tomorrow will be better, I'd hope when I finally collapsed in bed with the rise of the sun. Maybe I'd wake up and this knot in my chest would be gone, and I could take a deep breath without that spinning feeling in my belly.

But when I opened my eyes on a new day it was always more of the same from the one before.

Then one morning about three weeks after . . . that day . . . I was going through my clothes, thinking about just getting rid of some stuff, ya know? Well, I pulled out that blue suit, the one I'd worn to the church, and I felt the crackle of paper in the breast pocket of the jacket. I pulled it out. My stomach shifted, then settled. It was the poem I'd written for Nikita.

Finding my way to the edge of the bed, I opened the pages and began to read the words.

The afternoon I met her flashed before my eyes, our first kiss, the night she came to this same house, meeting her folks, me writing *A Private Affair,* coming back to New York, and marrying her. I saw our life together, the few years we had, short and bittersweet. Saw the night at the hospital, and the look on the savior's face when he told me how they'd tried to save her, and failed. I saw it all. I saw the words on the police report, *"Head on collision with truck at high speed. Truck ran red light . . . Grey Maxima totaled at the scene . . ."*

In front of me it ran like a high-speed video, full of flash and brilliant color but too brief to get the full effect, making you wanna play it again. And again.

Do it for you, I heard her say, the whispered words sounding like bubbles in her throat as she'd lain nearly motionless on the stretcher.

I read the lines on the pages again, and realized that I'd failed her in my promise. But it was just so damn hard. Hard to think about living when the life had been sucked out of me.

Life. Funny how it works, ya know? There are no guarantees, no prerequisites to making sure you pass its tests. You just take it and make it the best you can, hoping you won't fail.

That's what she wanted for me—always—to succeed, to go after all my dreams and make them real. But where could I begin again? I was tired—tired of starting over, picking up the pieces and making something out of nothing. Yeah, I still had my music—if I ever decided to play again. And Monica, Nikita's assistant at the publishing company, wanted me to decide what to do about the business. She said the authors and the staff were all holding their breath, waiting to see what I was going to do.

I wish I knew.

I stood, looked around, hoping to see something, anything, that would make a difference. Everything remained the same.

Walking toward the window, I looked out at the garden below. Our garden. I almost saw Nikita kneeling in the dirt, turning it with that little shovel. I heard the angry words we'd tossed at each other like stones that morning.

How many times since then had I wished that it had been different—that I'd said something else, hadn't walked out, had come home earlier? Ironic, *huh?* Talking about making a new life, and she lost hers. A sharp pain seared the center of my chest.

Maxine.

A child.

Ours.

Mine and hers.

The words, the scene with Max tap danced in my head, begging for attention, begging me to have the light shine down into the darkness of my mind so I could make it out, see what was really there.

I didn't want to believe Maxine—what she'd said. I couldn't, ya know? 'Cause I felt that if I did, if I believed, I would be dishonoring Nikita, somehow.

I wanted to believe that Maxine was lying, running a

game. But when my thoughts took that flight and made them land in my heart I knew that, as much as I didn't want to believe it, what Maxine told me that day in the cemetery was true. No matter how far I tried to run and hide from it, the truth was waiting right around the next corner—prepared to confront me.

A son. The life I'd been hoping for with Nikita was there with Maxine all along.

And as I stood there looking out at the garden, at my life, a slow–burning energy began to rev through my body, jump starting, then stopping, like an old car battery being charged after a long period of non–use.

I had a son. His name was Jamel. Maybe in some twisted way he was brought to me to replace the love I'd lost, give me something to hope for, dream about.

A son. Mine.

For the first time in three weeks, I got dressed and went out of the house. When I stepped outside, Mrs. Finch was in the yard sweeping, something she did religiously—even if there was nothing to sweep. I always figured it was just a way for her to check out the neighbors without looking as if she was.

"Quinten." She made a quick sign of the cross. "Son, my prayers have been answered." She propped her broom up against the steps and gave me a long hug with her bony arms.

Funny, it was the best feeling I'd had in a long time. I'd shut people out mentally and physically, and I hadn't realized until just then how much I missed the nearness and the caring. It was a gift that Nikita gave me. And I wanted to unwrap it again.

"Hey, Mrs. Finch. Come on, now. You're gonna break my back."

"Oh, you." She stepped back and smacked my arm, then moved slightly away and smiled up at me. Slowly, she bobbed her head up and down. "It's going to be all right now, son. I feel it."

"Thank you, ya know, for carin', lookin' out for me." I shrugged, still feeling shaky whenever I had to speak on how I felt.

"That's what you do when you love someone, Quinten. You try to make life easy and good for them. Think about their concerns and happiness."

"I didn't want to interfere with you finally finding happiness." I heard Maxine's words, and now maybe I understood why she'd said them, understood what she meant.

"Yeah, no doubt, Ms. Finch."

"Where are you headed? Because if you're going near a store, I need you to pick up a few things for me."

I tossed my head back and roared with laughter. Mrs. Finch never missed a beat. It must have been killing her not to be able to get me to run from one end of town to the other to "pick up a few things," for her. But, ya know, it felt damned good—laughing again, being needed again.

"I just gotta make a quick run 'cross town. I should be back in about an hour. So while I'm gone, get your list together and I'll take care of it when I get back."

She gave me a long, suspicious look. "It's not going to take you all day now, is it? 'Cause I just need a few things."

"I promise. Two hours, tops."

"All right, now. You go so you can come back soon. It's good to hear you laugh again." She stroked my cheek.

I could feel her eyes following me as I walked out of the gate toward my car, like a mom watching her kid go off to school, out to face the world. It felt good.

When I looked back over my shoulder she was standing there, a gentle smile on her face. I waved, got in the car and drove off.

It was good to be behind the wheel again. I had a sense of control, something that had been missing for the past weeks, a feeling of choice, of which road to take. The power was in my hands.

As the streets unfolded in front of me—honking horns, women darting in front of traffic with baby strollers daring me to hit them, brothers hanging out on the corners, music blasting from open windows—it all wrapped its arms around me in a form of welcome.

The beat, the rhythm, that had eluded me began to pump through my veins again, giving life like the fluid of an intravenous tube, feeding nourishment to its patient. And I took it all in, every drop.

I wasn't sure what my destination was. I was simply driving, you know? Taking in the scenes, breathing the air.

When I got uptown from The Village, cruising down One hundred Twenty–fifth street, along Amsterdam Avenue, over on St. Nicholas and across One hundred Thirty–fifth, I spotted plenty of folks I knew. Sometimes I stopped to kick it for a minute, most times I didn't. Just blew the horn and kept rolling. I wasn't quite ready for too much conversation. But this was a start.

I drove by Shug's Fish Fry and, as always, the line was out the door. You'd think Shug was giving fish away for free. But the real deal was, Shug's had the best fried whiting in all of Harlem. If the line hadn't been so long, I would've stopped for a taste, myself. For old time's sake.

I stopped by one of Remy's spots, just to let him know everything was cool with me, but he wasn't there. I did get to see Smalls, the house bouncer, who was still just as physically buffed and verbally silent as always.

Not sure where to go next, I thought about going back to the crib, then quickly tossed that thought. I'd been revived from a deep sleep, and I didn't want to run the risk of being seduced by that illicit drug—melancholia—again. At least not right now, especially when I thought about the real reason that had propelled me out of the doors of my crib and back out into the world.

As I drew closer to Central Park, I decided to find a parking space and maybe take a stroll along one of the trails, try to think some things through, decide what to do.

Walking along one of the paths, I tried to open myself up to the sights, sounds and smells around me, the same way I did when I sat down to compose a new song or craft a chapter in a book. That always cleared my head, making it easy for something new to come in and grow.

The air was cool, and the taste of the oncoming fall was there waiting patiently for its turn to take center stage, gently pushing the warmth of the summer aside. Shorts and T–shirts had been replaced by light jackets and long pants. Bright green began to retreat into the background, replaced in spots by gold and orange.

Couples walked closer than they had only weeks earlier, as if to absorb each others' heat.

Children ran across the grass, which was more crisp now than moist, the sounds of crackling leaves and fallen branches snapping like finger pops beneath their sneakered feet.

I took a sit down on a bench just opposite a playing field where a group of young boys were playing super heroes with an assortment of action figures. I smiled and stretched my arms across the back of the warped and weatherbeaten wood bench, and simply watched. Fascinated.

I wondered what kind of toys my son liked to play with. Did he have a little friend? Was he in school? What was his favorite food?

Maxine would know all that stuff. Stuff I'd missed out on, I thought, that sensation of anger easing its way through my head. I pushed the thoughts aside. What kind of mother was she? I almost saw a picture of her running across the grass with a little boy right behind her. Knowing Maxine, she took no shorts. If motherhood was the thing she wanted, she'd give it her absolute best—just like everything else in her life.

She been like that as long as I'd known her. The only other female I knew while we were growing up that was more determined than Maxine was my sister Lacy. Once either of them set their minds to something, it was on.

Man, I remember when Max first told me she was going to own a travel agency—all hers. She wound up working two jobs to make it happen. And when Lacy was killed, the jaws of life couldn't have pried Max away from finding out what really happened. She was the one who finally convinced me to pursue it from a legal standpoint.

It was Maxine who was there for me during those horrific times. There for me when the settlement came and I broke down. There for me even while I wrote *A Private Affair*, the story about me and Nikita. Maxine Sherman was an incredible woman.

I shut my eyes, bringing my hands to my chin. All my life I'd taken it for granted that Maxine would always be there, no matter what—accepting the deal with a smile and an open heart.

I'd been so angry with her these past weeks, since the day at the cemetery, so angry I didn't want to think about her or what she'd told me.

But as I allowed myself to think about her now, with an open mind, remembering the decent person she was, the hardness around my heart began to soften.

Could I really blame her for not telling me about Jamel? No. Maxine was too caring a person to intentionally hurt anyone. She thought she was doing the right thing—thinking of me and my life without putting herself first. How many other women would have done the same thing? Not many. I cringed, thinking about the ugly things I'd said to her.

And as much as I might want to be angry, feel betrayed by what she'd done, I couldn't help but admire her and her courage.

There had been a time when I'd wondered what my life

would have been like if Max and I had stayed together. *Choices.*

I stood, looked one last time at the kids who were beginning to disperse, taken home by their parents.

It was time I saw my son—took my responsibility, carried the weight. Maxine deserved that, and my son deserved his father. I had the chance to be the man my father never was to me. And maybe this was the starting over that would finally make the difference. I think Nikita would have understood.

MAXINE

FOURTEEN

Trying To Make It Right

It was Saturday—about noon—but outside it appeared as if night had fallen. A dark gloom hung like a heavy cloak over the entire city. There was a decided chill in the air. It had been raining relentlessly for two days—nonstop—and we were beginning to get cabin fever.

Jamel was restless and cranky, and wouldn't stop asking to go to McDonald's. Taylor had taken up what seemed like permanent residence in the recliner, smack in front of the television, mesmerized by one sport activity after another.

There was nothing left for me to clean, and I'd cooked enough food to last us through a recession.

I pushed the kitchen curtain aside from the window that opened onto our backyard. Everything was covered in a layer of water that rose to several inches in spots. The rain pop–popped, and ran in blinding sheets, hitting the ground so hard it bounced back up.

I wasn't quite sure if the weather had dampened my spirits, or something unseen. I had a disturbing feeling of unease—the way movie characters seem to feel when they sense danger stalking them from room to room.

I shook my head, trying to scatter the dark thoughts of dread, but I couldn't dispel the knot that had been building in the center of my chest since I'd gotten up that morning.

"Every time I feel like that, something's about to happen," I remember Lacy saying to me as we'd sat on her rickety, single bed reading magazines. "Like a pop quiz, or a shut off notice from the light company, or a fight. But it's always something."

"What do you do when you feel like that?" I'd asked her.

"Put it in God's hands. 'Cause whatever it is, until I know what it is there's nothing I can do about it."

That was one thing about Lacy—she was a devout believer in God and the power of prayer.

I was never what you would call religious, but I'd had my faith tried and tested on many occasions. There had been times when I just *knew* I couldn't keep my life together, but then I'd find the will and the strength, and there was a part of me that knew a higher power had a lot to do with my survival.

I let out a long sigh. Maybe I'd just follow Lacy's advice— 'Let go and let God,'—not worry over something I knew nothing about, and hopefully push aside this misty shadow that had been trailing me.

When I turned away from the window Taylor was standing in the doorway, cradling Jamel in his arms. A flood of warmth spread through me when I looked at them. So easy. So comfortable. So right.

"He finally wore himself out," Taylor said in a hush. "I'm going to put him to bed."

"Don't forget to pat his back for a minute—"

"Yes, mother hen," he kidded, cutting me off, "Or he'll pop right back up." He smiled indulgently at me. "I've been doing this for three years. Remember? Got it down to a science."

"Fine, smarty, but—"

"I know, don't forget to leave his door cracked and the hall light on in case he wakes up," he said, snatching the words before I could utter them.

"That's why I love you, Taylor Collins. I can just think the thoughts and you put them into words. My job here is done, ladies and gentlemen."

The corner of his mouth curved. "That's what you think. With little man out of the way for a minute, I have some thoughts I want you to put into action. Think you can handle it?"

I raised my chin and looked at him from beneath my lashes. "I've been doing it for three years. Remember?" I tossed back, full of sass and provocativeness.

His eyes momentarily darkened and a come–hither expression moved across his face. "Hold that thought."

Anticipation wound its way through my body, making me tingle with need while I watched him walk away.

Things had been great between Taylor and me since I'd returned from New York, at least after the first few days.

Initially, even after we'd made love that first night, things were a bit strained. We were overly polite, cautious of infringing on each other's space, just overdoing it, I guess in the belief that those things would make life between us magically return to normal. That wasn't what turned things around and got us back on track, though.

One night, about a week after I'd gotten back, we were in the kitchen cleaning up after dinner. Taylor was washing the dishes and I was drying. Since I never remembered to wear gloves, Taylor insisted on doing anything that had to do with harsh water. "As fine as you are, Girl," he'd said to me when we were in the early stages of the live–in life, "you need beautiful, soft hands to go with the rest of you."

That was just one of the many things that made him so special—he made me feel special and cherished and had no problem showing it, unlike so many other men who didn't, or couldn't.

Well, anyway, we were in the kitchen that night and I'd dropped the dishtowel. We bent to get it at the same time, and bumped heads.

After a volley of "I'm sorrys," "Excuse me's," and "Are you all right's," we looked at each other, really looked. Hunched down on the floor, rubbing our heads, we both realized, almost at the same instant that *this—this moment* was what we were all about. *Us.* Working together, loving each other, caring about each other. That's what was important.

We started to giggle. Then full out laughter consumed us until we sat on the floor hugging each other, the laughter cleansing us as pure as a summer shower.

"I guess we should knock each other in the head more often," he said when we'd finally pulled ourselves together.

"I know that things can't be exactly as they were, Taylor. And I think that's why we've been tiptoeing around these past days, not wanting to disturb the tenuous peace. But what has always been the bedrock of our relationship is our ability to be open with each other and share our feelings."

He curved his arm a bit tighter around my shoulders, pulling me closer against him. "I know, and when that broke down so did a level of trust and security. To me it feels like I'm walking across a tightrope, Max, no longer sure if the safety net is under me."

"Why, baby?"

He sighed, his gaze taking in the room as if he could locate the answer he was searching for. "From the day I committed myself to you, Jamel, and this relationship, I never looked back. Never for one minute did I have any doubts about us. But when all this happened, and especially the way it did, it shook me. And to tell the truth I still feel a bit shaky."

"Do you think I'm still in love with Quinn? Is that it?"

"Honestly?"

"Yes. Honestly."

"Jamel is not only your son. He's Quinn's son, too. He's the link to a past you'll never get away from, Max. That's reality. And he's also a part of who we are—our tie. What if Quinn fights for custody? What then? What if the only way not to lose your son is to go back to him?"

The same questions had haunted me. What if? What would I do?

"My prayer is that it won't come to that, to a point where I'm forced to choose because it would be a long and ugly fight. I won't give up my son, and I won't loose you in the process of keeping him. But the reality is, it could come to that. All I can say, from the bottom of my heart, is that if we, you and I, are in this together, if I know I have your support and love, we'll work through it. And whatever is best for Jamel, first and foremost, will be the deciding factor. I can't be anymore honest than that."

"That's all I want, Maxine. The rest of it I can handle. And I want you to know that Jamel's happiness is just as important to me. I would never stand in the way of that. No matter what."

When I looked into his eyes I knew without a doubt what love really was, and understood that Taylor's love for me and Jamel knew no bounds.

No one can ever understand what it feels like to know you are loved like that unless you've experienced it. I consider myself among the lucky, chosen few. All I could hope for was to be able to give back to him all that he'd given me.

The sound of his footsteps coming back down the stairs pulled me back from that turning moment. As I moved away from the window heading for the living room, wanting to meet him halfway, the phone rang.

I answered the kitchen wall phone.

"Hello?"

"Maxine? This is Q."

A jolt—the kind of sensation that rushes through you when an elevator drops several floors—assaulted me, arresting my breath.

"Quinn," I finally uttered.

"I, *uh*, know this call must be a shock. Glad your number didn't change. It's been a while."

I cleared my throat, tried to find my voice as Taylor's footsteps approached. "Yes, it has been. How is everything?"

"Gettin' there. Day by day."

We were both silent for a moment. The music coming from the living room stereo, which Taylor must have put on, was the only sound above the rapid racing of my heart.

"So—how have you been, Max? I know we didn't part on good terms."

"I'm okay." I looked over my shoulder and could see Taylor through the doorway, sifting through our collection of CDs.

"I'm sorry about all that, ya know," he said. "Caught me off guard. I—didn't mean those things I said to you, Max. Really."

"It's all right. I understand."

"Do you? I kind of knew you would. You always understood me."

Silence.

"I've been thinkin', ya know, that I should take a trip out there so we could talk. Me and you—work somethin' out. And, ya know, I could get to meet my son. He should know who I am."

I felt a thin line of perspiration break out along my hairline as I tried to sort through the array of scenarios he'd tossed at me—Us, talk? Meet Jamel? My tomorrow had arrived today. The room began to shrink.

"Quinn, I—"

"You told him about me, right? Who his father is?"

I took a steadying breath. "No. I haven't."

"Max!" Taylor called, and I covered the mouthpiece. "Come on, woman. I know that must be Marva, for you to be chatting so long. I'm missing you. No telling how long little man will sleep."

In one ear I heard Quinn's angry question—his voice bubbling like hot lava—and Taylor's sweet entreaty in the other.

"Answer me, Maxine. Why haven't you told him about me? He *is* mine. That's what you said."

My chest tightened. I heard the near desperate tone in his voice, something so foreign for Quinn, as if the answer was somehow his lifeline, what he'd been holding onto to stay afloat.

"Everything I told you is true," I finally said.

"So what's the problem?"

"There is none." I pulled in some air, then let everything out in a rush. "I never knew if I'd ever see you again, Quinn, if Jamel would ever see you—or when."

"What are you sayin'? Don't play with me, Maxine. What are you sayin'?"

"Jamel doesn't know about you because he's grown up thinking' that Taylor is his father."

There was dead silence. For a moment I thought he'd hung up.

"You have some other man *pretendin'* to be my son's father? That's what you're tellin' me?"

"He's not—"

"You came to New York to tell me all that b.s. and knew

what you were doin' all along? Is this about hurtin' me, Max? Gettin' back at me for leavin' you? Is that the deal?''

"Quinn. Just listen to me. Please.''

"Why? So you can tell me some more mess that I'm supposed to suck up? What can you tell me now? Huh?''

"First of all, you have to calm down so that I can explain.''

"Ain't nothin' to explain, Maxine. I'm not tryin' to hear it. Whatever it is you've done, you deal with it. I'm out. But check this, if he is my son, one of these days he'll want to know the real deal. What story will you tell then?''

The sound of the phone slamming clanged in my ear.

For several moments I simply stood there, the phone clutched in my hand, pressed to my ear, the sound of the dial tone humming—the connection broken.

"Max, you okay, Baby?''

I turned, stunned. I hadn't heard Taylor come up behind me.

"Max?'' He put his hand on my shoulder. "Who was that?''

Even though he asked the question, something in his eyes and the tone of his voice told me he already knew.

"Quinn.''

For a split second he shut his eyes and let out a breath— the kind you exhale when you finally accept the inevitable.

He took the phone from my hand and hung it up. "What did he say?''

I shook my head, then lowered it before slowly replaying my conversation with Quinn. When I'd finished, Taylor turned away and walked to the other side of the kitchen. The table separated us. He braced his hands on the back of the chair.

"Max, I have to tell you I don't like this. I don't like the feeling I'm getting. And I don't like the fact that Jamel is going to get caught in the middle.''

I crossed my arms beneath my breasts. "He's just upset, that's all," I said finally, scrambling for a response.

"This isn't going to go away, Maxine. You know that."

"I know," I mumbled, crossing the space to take a seat at the table.

"At some point we're going to have to say something to Jamel."

I looked up from staring at my hands. "No." I shook my head. "He's too young to understand."

"Maxine, both of us have created this little world, where we're this perfect family. And maybe looking from the outside we are. But inside—all is not perfect, Max. And we can't go blindly along thinking that it is. We've got to take responsibility for the way things are."

"Don't you think I know that?" I snapped, my frustration and confusion hurled at the easiest target, accompanied by a bolt of lightning that lit the darkened afternoon sky like fireworks. "That's why I went to New York, to get things out in the open. I could have stayed here and kept living my life as it's been, but the time for airing the laundry was going to come, no matter how long I tried to wait it out."

"So now what? We just sit back and wait for our life to be pulled out from under us? I know that's not what you're saying."

"No, it's not." All at once the murky picture became perfectly clear. I walked around to his side of the table, and stood in front of him. "You're the only father Jamel has ever known. Maybe we were wrong to have him believe you're his natural father. But the fact is, what's done is over. We're a family. We are Jamel's parents in every sense of the word. And if Quinn is even half the man I know him to be, what will come first before his pride, before his pain, will be doing what's right for Jamel—when it's right. And when he comes—you and I will make sure that he leaves understanding that."

Taylor took my face in his hands and gazed down into my eyes. His voice flowed through me like the chorus of a spiritual. "That's all I want to hear."

His mouth covered mine in a slow drag kiss, sealing our pact and the future that lay ahead.

QUINN

FIFTEEN

My Turn Now

I got Sean Michaels, my attorney, on the phone right after I hung up with Maxine. Sean was the one who'd finally gotten the city to admit what they'd done and pay for the wrongful death of my sister, Lacy. I trusted Sean, which was something rare for me, I thought, as I listened to the Muzak while his secretary paged him.

I knew I was running on pure adrenaline, not thinking clearly, not planning, but I felt like a runaway train, totally crazed and out of control. How could she have done that to me—erased me as if I didn't exist? Jamel was my son. I knew it, even if I had thrown doubt in the air like loose change dumped on a dresser top. Maxine wouldn't lie to me. Not about something like that. That's why I couldn't understand why she would disrespect me that way. It wasn't like Maxine, at least not the Maxine I knew.

"Quinn? How are things?" Sean asked, coming onto the phone.

"Gettin' there."

"Good. It'll take some time. What can I do for you? New contract?"

"Naw. Nothing like that. It's personal. I want to stop by your office and run a few things by you."

"Sure. When did you want to stop by?"

"I could be there in forty minutes, tops."

"Oh. I didn't realize you meant today. Sounds serious."

"It is."

"I'll rearrange some things and I'll see you when you get here."

"Thanks, Sean. See you in a few."

I wasn't sure what Sean could do, but a gut feeling told me he could do something—or at least act on whatever my decision was. And I damn sure wanted to have this whole issue with Jamel and Maxine—and the guy, whoever he was—cleared up quick and in a hurry.

As I felt the purr of my car engine beneath me and the power I always experienced behind the wheel, a sudden rush of fury vibrated through me. My whole world was on tilt. The one person who'd kept me grounded and focused was gone, and the one thing I'd wanted more than anything was in the hands of someone else. *Nikita. Jamel.*

I was mad. Mad at everyone, at life. Yeah, I might have done some things back in the day. Stuff I'd rather forget about. But was this my payback? Did I really deserve this?

I turned onto the F.D.R. Drive and headed downtown. Then all at once I heard Nikita, as clearly as if she sat right next to me. "You need to be careful how you live your life, Quinn. It will come back to haunt you."

Blinking, I shook off the chill that had crept up my spine.

Guess she was right in a way. I'd made decisions, some not so good, but they were mine. For the most part I tried to do the right thing by folks, as long as they were straight with me. But, as Remy had taught me since I was sixteen—

years—old, "Business is business. Don't take no shorts." Yeah, words to live by. And that's exactly what I intended to do. This thing between Maxine and me was all about getting our business straight, and me getting what was mine. My son. Whatever it took.

Pulling up in front of Sean's office building, I looked up at the window of the floor where I knew his office was, and remembered the first time I'd come there.

It was Maxine who'd hooked up the meeting and insisted that I go and see what Sean and his wife Khendra could do about getting the New York City Police Department to admit what really happened to Lacy the night she was killed. It took them months to break down the blue wall of silence and finally get them to cough up a six figure settlement—hush money—but all the money in the world couldn't ever make up for the hole that her death had left in my soul. I took part of the money and launched the Lacy Parker Foundation to help underprivileged kids get started in the music business—from purchasing instruments to voice lessons and music classes, to supporting music programs in some of the inner city schools. In other words, black schools in poor neighborhoods. I think Lacy would have been happy about that.

The thing is, if not for Maxine bugging me and insisting that something could be done, convincing me that we had an obligation to Lacy to make things right, I don't know what would have happened to me, what I would have done. She was the thread that held me together—my friend, supporter, and finally lover.

Now, there I was, right back where it all started nearly six years ago, making moves to get my son from the woman who'd been instrumental in helping me keep my sanity.

I stepped out of the car and pulled my leather jacket a bit tighter around my body, warding off the chilly breeze. One of my locks came loose from the band that held them in place and whipped around my face. Fall was definitely here.

I heard the telltale beep of the alarm kicking into place. I rounded the front of the car and headed for the building, grabbed the chrome handle on the door and pulled it open. *Funny how things work out,* I thought.

Didn't have to wait long before I met with Sean. Too bad his reaction was far from what I expected.

"Quinn. You know as well as I do that there's due process. You can't go charging out there and take him away from his mother. Besides, before you can claim any rights you need to prove he's your son."

I jumped up from my seat and put my face close enough to his to see the pores in his skin. He didn't flinch.

"Look, Man, she told me he was mine! That's all I need to know. Get him. I pay you to take care of my business. So do what I pay you to do."

I knew I was pushing it. This wasn't the way I operated with my friends. I could hear the venom in my voice, but I didn't care. I needed this. *Had* to have it. And I didn't give a damn how much it cost, or what had to be done to make it happen. Jamel was all I had now. I couldn't step back and have him taken from me, too. No. I wasn't having it.

Sean stood. His voice stayed at that courtroom low, which only seemed to escalate my emotions.

"I may be your attorney, Quinn, but I'm also your friend. This is not the way to handle it. You've been under a lot of strain lately, with Niki and now this. You're not thinking clearly."

"So what are you sayin'? I'm off the edge? I know what I want, Sean. My son. Period. End of story. And if you can't or won't make that happen, then I'll handle it myself."

I spun away, stalking toward the door, my anger and raw emotion nearly blinding me. My head pounded.

"Don't do it, Quinn."

The words slowed my steps, but didn't stop me.

I drove around for a while, with no real direction. It felt as if everything was slipping away again. Just when I'd gotten my fingertips on the life jacket it got pulled away by the tide of circumstance, and I was being dragged by the undertow. The glimmer that I had something to strive for, something that was mine, was all that kept me afloat these past days. Now the light at the end of this painfully dark road was growing dim.

But I refused to drown. I wasn't going out like that. I was tired of being the victim. The only times things worked for me was when I took matters into my own hands, just like I did when I started working for Remy to make enough loot to take care of me and Lacy. Yeah, the work was on the dark side, and I took a lot of chances walking up on folks in the street, back rooms, and tenement hallways and demanding they pay what they owed, or else. But I did what was necessary, the only thing I could do at the time.

And I took chances playing the baby grand in Nick's club, *Rhythms*, and taking the gig he offered me as a result of hearing me play, then going back to school to master my craft. But I did it. I made music, with him and on my own.

It was risky of me to write my first book. Black men writing love stories were pretty much unheard of, then. But *A Private Affair* opened new worlds for me, personally and professionally.

But the greatest risk of all was marrying Nikita Harrell, a Cornell medical student from black suburbia, with the secret aspiration of being a girl from the 'hood. Stepping into her world of the black bourgeoise was like walking into a house of mirrors. I could never tell if what I was seeing and living was the real thing or only a reflection of something else.

It was through her that the true test of me as a man was taken. Everything I thought I was about was brought into question. The tough, unreachable, silent man couldn't play in her game of life. She challenged me to break down my stereotyped wall and face what was inside and not run from what I saw.

I told her once, early in our relationship, "You bring out the melody in a man." And I meant that. Nikita allowed me to be all that I could be.

So now here I was, a man who had finally learned how to love, how to accept it and give it in return, and I had no one to share myself with—except my son. And I wouldn't let anything or anyone stop me. I was going to San Francisco, and I was going for my son. And for myself.

After making flight arrangements and tossing some clothes in a bag, I headed for Kennedy Airport. I was booked on the last flight of the day.

Once I was on the plane it really hit me about what I was doing. Things slowly came into focus. My heart was no longer racing, and words of caution from Sean and then Nick vibrated in my head.

"You need to relax and chill a minute," Nick had said when I'd stopped by the club on the way home, to tell him what I was planning.

"Three years is long enough to chill, don't you think, Man?" I ran my fingers across the keys of the piano. The tinkling sound danced off the walls of the empty club. Happy Hour would bring folks in by the carloads, I'd thought absently.

"Q, listen. You running off half–cocked is going to cause more problems than it solves. Sean is right. Due process, Brother. Handle this correctly, or you might blow it."

I glanced sideways at him. I let him talk, but I wouldn't let the words get to me. He didn't know how I felt, what was going on inside of me, what I needed to fill the gaps. 'Cause if he did, we wouldn't have had those crazy conversations. The book I was writing could wait. Finishing up in the studio and preparing for the tour could wait. Deciding what to do about Nikita's publishing company could wait. I had to settle this before I could begin to think about the rest of my life.

By the time the plane landed six hours later in California, whatever doubts that had crept under my skin were exorcised. I'd made the trip for one reason, and one reason alone. And I was more determined than ever to satisfy the need I'd come to fill.

It was after midnight on a Friday when I finally got checked in and settled in my hotel room. My plan was to see Maxine first thing in the morning. No more phone calls. I figured she couldn't put me off if we were face–to–face. Plus, I didn't want her to have the opportunity to tell me no.

My guess was that she was still living in the same place we'd shared, since her phone number hadn't changed. The thought that she might have moved glided momentarily through my head as I unpacked, but I wouldn't let it land. If she wasn't there I'd just deal with it when the time came.

The idea that she was sharing that house with another man suddenly hit me, and quick rush of male ego took root.

What was the deal with that? I wondered. Was she married to the guy or were they just living together, as we had been? What kind of man was he that would take on the role of father, knowing that the child wasn't his? Or did he think Jamel was his son?

Naw. I nixed that last question. Maxine wasn't like that. I couldn't imagine her running that kind of game on someone.

I knew Maxine. Or at least I thought I did. But I also knew we'd both changed in the years we'd been apart. I had to be prepared for a side of Maxine I'd never known—Maxine the mother.

Undressed and stretched out on the queen–size hotel

bed, I played around with a variety of scripts: the conversation with Max, meeting my son and telling him who I was; bringing him back to New York with me and showing him my world; making a life for us.

I thought about those things until I couldn't think anymore, and finally dozed off.

When I opened my eyes the next day, it took me a minute to realize where I was and why I was in a strange room. Then it all came back.

I took a quick shower and got dressed, planning my outfit carefully. I wanted to give the right impression. This was business, but it was also very personal, so I decided semi–casual was in order. The open–necked, white cotton shirt and gray slacks gave just the right effect I was looking for. I tied my locks back with my trust, black band, and I was ready.

The bell captain flagged down a cab for me and we took off.

"Thirty–six eighty–four Palisades Drive," I said, and sat back.

"Hmm. Nice neighborhood. Great place to raise a family."

A twinge gripped my chest. I ignored him, or tried to.

"Used to live in New York, myself," he went on. "What a hellhole. Had to get my kids out of there. The school system sucks, gangs taking over neighborhoods. And the expense. *Whew!* I mean, it's expensive out here, too, but at least you get some decoration to go with it. Look at that."

He angled his chin in the direction of the Golden Gate Bridge.

It gleamed like a king's ransom against the morning sunshine and rippling waves of water. It was an unusual day for Frisco. The sky was virtually smog–free, and you could see for miles. Riding around when I lived out here, I wrote some of my best music, and the scenes from my book came together many a day as I walked up and down the rolling streets and wandered in and out of shops.

Although it was a big city, it still had a small town feel. You didn't get the sense of being swallowed, like in New York.

"You're not from here. I can tell," the cabby said, moving my thoughts out of the way.

"Naw. Not really. Lived here for a while."

"What made you leave?"

I looked out toward the horizon. "A woman."

He chuckled. "That'll do it. So you're just visiting, I take it. Or are you planning to come back to stay?"

"Visit."

We stopped for a red light and I saw him staring at me in the rearview mirror. His dark eyes squinted for a minute. "You sure look familiar," he said kind of slowly, as if he'd have the answer by the time he got all the words out.

"Naw, I doubt it."

He was still staring at me. Then he popped his fingers. "I know. You're that musician whose wife was killed in a car accident. It was in all the papers. Real sad. Real sad. Sorry about your wife. That must have been hard."

I didn't answer. I just wanted to get out. *Success.*

"Yeah, yeah, I remember now. You two have any kids? They didn't mention it in the paper, but that doesn't mean anything. They get things wrong all the time. Kids have a way of anchoring you, you know? *Do* you have kids?"

For an instant I was torn. I did have a son. But not with my wife. To say yes would imply that Nikita and I had children. To say no would negate Jamel's existence. More importantly, it wasn't any of his business.

"I'd rather not talk anymore if you don't mind." I rolled down the window even though the air–conditioning was on, to let some outside noise in.

For the rest of the ride we drove in silence, which gave

me a chance to really pay attention to what the old man had said.

Where I grew up in New York, smack in the middle of Harlem, gangs, shoot—outs, holdups, drugs, were as commonplace as getting the mail. Even though I was able to get out, I knew the kind of toll it could take—especially on black boys.

The neighborhood I lived in now was pretty cool. The Village had its problems, no doubt, like anyplace else, but for the most part it wasn't bad.

Could I bring a kid up there? I didn't know. What about touring, playing at clubs, late-night rehearsals? How would I manage, alone, with a small child? The thoughts settled like a rock in the pit of my stomach.

I looked up, and we were pulling onto Maxine's street. A flood of memories filled me—all the times I'd walked in and out of that door, spent my days and nights in those rooms. It was almost like a dream now, part of something I could no longer grasp. And I knew the realities behind that door were far removed from anything I'd experienced there.

"That'll be twelve—fifty," the driver grumbled, no longer my chatty companion.

I pulled a twenty out of my wallet and handed it to him. "Keep the change," I mumbled and stepped out. He couldn't drive away fast enough. Guess he thought I was going to change my mind about the tip.

For a couple of minutes I stood there on the street, staring at the house, no longer certain of what I was walking into. But whatever the deal, I must be prepared.

I walked up the steps, rang the bell, and had a sudden urge for a cigarette. I could almost taste it. I clasped my hands in front of me to keep from reaching for the pack in the pocket of my shirt.

"Just a minute," I heard a male voice shout. I straightened. Ready.

Seconds later the door was pulled open and a tall, slender brother—the kind usually seen on the pages of magazines in sportswear ads—answered the door.

Before he even asked I realized he knew who I was. I could tell from the tiny flicker at the corner of his eye, and the way his nostrils flared a bit when he took a breath.

"Yes?" he asked, playing it off, hoping I was the cable guy and not the last person he wanted to see.

"I'm Quinn Parker. I came to see Maxine."

He looked at me for a moment, and whatever hope he had moments ago vanished.

"Maxine's not here."

His gaze silently challenged mine. I gave it right back.

"She should be home soon. You want to come in and wait?"

That was the last thing I expected him to say, and I worked hard at keeping my expression neutral.

I shrugged. "How long do you think she'll be?"

"Maybe an hour. Maybe less."

"I could come back."

"Hey, it's up to you."

"Daddy!"

My heart pounded against my chest as if it wanted to get out. Taylor turned toward the sound of the voice coming from behind him and I caught a glimpse of a little boy running down the foyer.

So many emotions grabbed me at once: excitement, fear, doubt, pride, all jockeying for position. As he drew nearer I could feel my insides swell, my throat clench. He looked at me—the same dark eyes and sharp nose. I remember my mother saying once that we had Indian in our blood. But the full lips and the smile were Maxine all the way. It was the most awesome feeling I'd ever had. This was my son. A part of me. No doubt.

Unconsciously I made a move toward him as he

approached, pulled by some unseen string, but he went straight for Taylor, who hoisted him up in his arms.

"Told you about running down the hall, short–stop," he said in a calm but firm tone, the kind parents use when they scold their kids in front of company. I had a feeling that's the way Taylor always talked to Jamel, firm but loving. Something inside me twisted. "I don't want you to hurt yourself," he added.

Jamel stuck his finger in his mouth and rested his head on Taylor's shoulder. "Who's that?" I heard him mumble over his thumb.

Taylor gave me a quick glance laced with warning. "He's a friend of your mommy."

Jamel stared at me. "Hi," he said.

My throat tightened. "Hi," I forced myself to say.

"Do you want to wait?" Taylor asked again.

I blinked and focused on him, looked at my son cradled in Taylor's arm as if he belonged there—Jamel looking so much like me but not knowing who I was. An ache built inside my chest, wanting to explode. I pushed the pain away. "Yeah, I'll wait."

He stepped aside to let me pass, still holding Jamel close to his body.

When I walked through the door I was instantly thrown back in time. The rooms were like I remembered them, sunny and bright. Plants, Max's favorite things, were everywhere, more than I recalled from when I lived there. The furniture was still in the same places, but the pieces had been replaced. The stereo was definitely new, and I didn't remember the television being quite so large. And the rooms had a new coat of paint. Funny—the same but different.

I crossed the living room to the mantle and looked at a row of framed photographs. There were a few of Maxine tucked under Taylor's arm, looking really happy, smiling at each other, but most of them were of Jamel at different stages of his life, the years I'd missed. The one that struck me the hardest was a picture of the three of them.

I stepped closer and picked it up. It was a typical Sears family portrait. The three of them—Maxine on one side, Taylor on the other, and Jamel between them. I tried to see myself there, fit myself in, but the picture got too crowded.

"Want something to drink while you're waiting?"

Taylor's voice jerked me back. I returned the picture to the mantle and turned toward him, jamming my hands into my pants pockets, suddenly feeling like a sneak thief.

"Naw. Thanks."

We looked at each other for a minute—two men who'd shared the same house, the same woman, the same child, neither willing to back down and give the other his space.

"You know I came for my son," I said, needing to get that out, get it straight.

His gaze narrowed. I saw his jaw clench. "It's not that simple, and don't think it is, not for a minute."

"I can take care of him. You and Maxine have each other, you can have more kids."

"We already have a kid, Quinn."

"Maybe, but I'm a part of that whether you want to accept it or not. He needs to know who I am. And I'm gonna be a part of his life. A major part."

"And how do you intend to do that, Quinn—by uprooting him, taking him away from everything he knows and loves to satisfy your own needs? What about his?"

"Kids adjust." I knew I'd had to.

"But at what cost?"

The question halted me for a minute, resurrecting my own fractured youth. "You tryin' to tell me to stay out of his life?"

"I'm telling you that there's a time for everything."

I laughed, a nasty chuckle. "You sound like Maxine." I saw him flinch. "When's the right time for you? When he's off to college, needs his first car, or when they're ready to put *me* six feet under? Huh? When's the right time, Taylor?"

"This isn't the way to solve it."

He crossed the room and sat down on the couch, thighs splayed, his forearms resting on them. "Listen, Man, I love that boy as if he were my own son. And I love Maxine. Their happiness comes first with me. This isn't a role I would have cut out for myself, but it's here and I'm in it for the duration." He blew out a breath and slowly shook his head. "You had your chance with Maxine. You made the choice to leave, and she made the choice to move on with her life."

"This ain't about Maxine."

"Oh, but it is. Very much so. Maxine is at the core of it all. She's Jamel's mother. She's provided the foundation for her son, for this family. She's the one who holds everything together."

We both turned at the sound of the front door closing.

"I'm back!" Maxine called out.

The sound of keys clanged against the table in the foyer.

I heard the rhythmic tap tap of her footsteps as she drew closer, then a second set, lighter, running down the stairs.

"Mommy!"

"Hey, sweetie," I heard her reply.

"Your friend here, Mommy."

Her voice grew closer.

"My friend?"

And then she was standing in the doorway with Jamel wrapped around her body like a scarf. Her expression froze when she saw me.

"Told you," Jamel chirped, hopping out of her arms and dashing to Taylor, who braced him between his thighs.

I saw her exposed throat work up and down like she was trying to unclog the words.

"Quinn," she finally uttered.

Her gaze slanted toward Taylor and Jamel, then swung back toward me, as if she were struggling with some decision.

She crossed the room and sat next to Taylor.

The invisible line was drawn.

"You should have called first," she said. "We weren't expecting you." She rested her hand on Taylor's thigh. Jamel sprinted away, back up the stairs at the sound of Scooby Doo coming from the television above us, but not before I saw the picture again. This time it was live and in living color—the three of them.

I continued to stand, not wanting to lose my edge but already knowing I had.

"I took a chance," I said in response to her statement about my untimely arrival. "I had some business to take care of in town," I lied, then shrugged keeping everyone's pride in tact, especially my own. "So I thought I'd stop by, ya know?"

"I—we don't want Jamel upset, Quinn. He's just a baby." I heard the tremor in her voice, and saw the pleading in her eyes.

All of a sudden I finally understood what Nikita had been saying all along. *Do it for you. Be everything you ever hoped for.* She didn't mean rise to stardom, take everything that came my way. She was telling me to be all the man I could be—a real man, willing to stand on my own two feet and do the right thing by those around me. For me. And being a man right then meant walking away, doing right by these people in front of me, doing right by my son, even though it was tearing me up inside. Deep down I knew I wasn't prepared to be what Jamel needed. He had that, here with them. A family. I wanted him to make up for what I'd lost, but that wasn't Jamel's responsibility. It was mine. I had to heal first, be whole again, before I could be a father, a friend. Nikita understood this all along. She knew and tried to tell me. She realized I wasn't ready to be a father. I was still learning how to be a partner, a husband, a man.

I looked at them both, at the rooms, listened to the sound of Jamel's laughter coming from upstairs. I remembered being there, living there. I no longer belonged in this place. Not anymore. Not in this picture.

Slowly I nodded. "My flight leaves in about two hours, and I still have that business to take care of," I said. "I guess I better get rollin'."

They both stood. Maxine walked up to me, stroked my cheek the way she used to. "Thank you," she whispered.

"You'll call, let me know how he's doing, if you need anything?"

She nodded. "Of course. And we'll work something out, Q, I promise you that. I just want Jamel to be prepared. Please understand. You will be a part of his life."

"Thanks." I turned to leave and they both followed me to the door. Just then Jamel came down the stairs.

"Come and say good–bye, Jamel," Maxine said.

He ambled over and looked up at me.

I squatted down and looked him in the eye, trying to memorize his face, the scent of him. "See ya," I said.

"See ya," he repeated.

"Can I get a hug?"

He looked up at his mother. She nodded.

Cautiously he stepped closer and I took him in my arms. I felt everything inside of me give way, and I shut my eyes. Reluctantly I released him. "You be a good guy, okay?"

" 'Kay."

I stood and exhaled, turned, and walked away.

EPILOGUE
ONE YEAR LATER
TAYLOR, MAXINE, QUINN

All In Good Time

It was our usual Saturday outing. Since Maxine and I married six months earlier we made it a family ritual to spend the day together. The afternoon was clear, almost crisp. I knew what I was about to do would be difficult, but it was the right thing, the right time. I pulled the car into the first parking space.

"We here, Daddy?" Jamel asked.

"Yes, Buddy. We're here." I got out while Maxine unbuckled him from his carseat. I rounded the car and took Jamel's hand. "Come on, Pop."

We walked toward the door, moving to the side as the crowd began filing out. With Jamel's hand in mine, I walked down the narrow aisle toward where the table was set up in the back.

The last of the autograph seekers shook Quinn's hand and moved away, clutching her treasure to her chest. He was alone, his focus concentrated on collecting his belongings, surrounded by his latest book, *Pieces of Dreams*.

"There's Mommy's friend, Daddy."

"And your friend, too, buddy," I said.

Quinn looked up, his hand poised. Slowly he stood. For a moment confusion hovered in the darkness of his gaze. Then understanding settled down, gentle as a feather floating to earth.

Jamel and I stepped closer.

"We thought it was time he saw what you did," I said to Quinn. "Get to know you."

A gentle smile of thanks spread across his face as he gazed from me to Jamel. Then he looked beyond me toward the door. I turned. There was Maxine framed in the archway. Slowly she approached, and the four of us stood together on the threshold of tomorrow.

Sometimes healing can begin with a simple gesture.

Dear Reader,

I hope you enjoyed entering the world of Maxine and Quinn once again, and meeting Taylor, who I believe epitomizes the depth and compassion of so many black men. For all the readers who read *A Private Affair*, I hope your questions and your need to know were finally answered!

The style of *Pieces of Dreams* is a bit different from the typical romance, but these characters were never typical, and I wanted to have the opportunity to have them speak directly to you, share their deepest emotions, and allow you to share in their growth. I hope I accomplished that. This story, as with many that I try to convey, speaks to issues so very prevalent in our society—ready–made families, and the roles and responsibilities of all the players. It is not easy, and many walk away when the going gets too tough, but even as painful as it was for Maxine, Quinn, and Taylor, they found a mature way to deal with a very difficult situation. I wish them all the best, as their chapter is finally closed.

Thank you all for your endless support, your letters and your e-mail. They keep my spirits lifted. I hope that all of you will tune into your BET network when *Intimate Betrayal*, *A Private Affair* and *Masquerade* are aired this fall. I'm thrilled, and anxiously await seeing Maxwell and Reese, Quinn and Wikita, and Joi and Marcus come to life on the screen. And I hope that all of you will make the journey with me to mainstream land when my next novel, *The Seduction of Innocence* is released in April.

I love hearing from you. You may write to me in care of Kensington Publishing, 850 Third Ave., N.Y., N.Y. 10022. Please include a legal–size self–addressed stamped envelope, or e-mail at dhill@queens.lib.ny.us

Once again, thank you for your love and support. Continued blessings to you all.

Until next time,

Donna

ABOUT THE AUTHOR

Bestselling and award–winner author Donna Hill began her writing career in 1987 with the short story, *The Long Walk*. Her first book, *Rooms of the Heart* was released in 1990, followed by the bestseller, *Indiscretions* in 1991. Both titles have been re–released after being out of print for several years. Since 1991, Donna has penned sixteen titles, three of which, *Intimate Betrayal, A Private Affair* and *Masquerade,* are scheduled as television movies, to be aired on the BET network in the fall of 1999. Coming in April of next year will be her first mainstream title published by Kensington Books, entitled, *The Seduction of Innocence.* Donna continues to pursue her public relations career with the Queens Library system, and lives in Brooklyn, New York with her family.

COMING IN JULY 1999 . . .

FIRE AND DESIRE,   (1-58314-020-7, $4.99/$6.50)
by Brenda Jackson
Geologist Corithians Avery, and head foreman of Madaris Explorations, Trevor Grant, are assigned the same business trip to South America. Each has bittersweet memories of a night two years ago when she walked in on him—Trevor half-naked and she wearing nothing more than a black negligee. The hot climate is sure to rouse suppressed desires.

HEART OF STONE,   (1-58314-025-5, $4.99/$6.50)
by Doris Johnson
Disillusioned with dating, wine shop manager Sydney Cox has settled for her a mundane life of work and lonely nights. Then unexpectedly, love knocks her down. Executive security manager Adam Stone enters the restaurant and literally runs into Sydney. The collision cracks the barriers surrounding their hearts . . . and allows love to creep in.

NIGHT HEAT.   (1-58314-026-3, $4.99/$6.50)
by Simona Taylor
When Trinidad tour guide Rhea De Silva is assigned a group of American tourists at the last minute, things don't go too well. Journalist Marcus Lucien is on tour to depict a true to life picture of the island, even if the truth isn't always pretty. Rhea fears his candid article may deflect tourism. But the night heat makes the attraction between the two grow harder to resist.

UNDER YOUR SPELL,   (1-58314-027-1, $4.99/$6.50)
by Marcia King-Gamble
Marley Greaves returns to San Simone for a job as research assistant to Dane Carmichael, anthropologist and author. Dane's reputation on the island has been clouded, but Marley is drawn to him entirely. So when strange things happen as they research Obeah practices, Marley sticks by him to help dispel the rumors . . . and the barrier around his heart.

Available wherever paperbacks are sold, or order direct from the Publisher. Send cover price plus 50¢ per copy for mailing and handling to BET Books, c/o Kensington Publishing Corp., Consumer Orders, or call (toll free) 888-345-BOOK, to place your order using Mastercard or Visa. Residents of New York, Washington D.C., and Tennessee must include sales tax. DO NOT SEND CASH.